THE DREAM YEARS

Lisa Goldstein

BANTAM BOOKS
TORONTO • NEW YORK • LONDON • SYDNEY • AUCKLAND
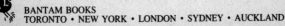

THE DREAM YEARS

A Bantam Book

Bantam Hardcover Edition / September 1985

Bantam Spectra edition / July 1986

Library of Congress Cataloging in Publication Data

Goldstein, Lisa
    The dream years.

    1. Breton, Andre, 1896–1966, in fiction, drama,
poetry, etc. I. Title
PS3557.0397D7 1985   813'.54   85-7458
    ISBN 0-553-25693-9

Published simultaneously in the United States and Canada

PRINTED IN THE UNITED STATES OF AMERICA

O   0 9 8 7 6 5 4 3 2 1

Many people helped with the writing of this book, among them Doug Asherman, Ira Bernstein, Jeff Mariotte, Dennis Hanson and the crew at Books, Inc. in San Jose, Lou Aronica, Dave Hartwell, Richard Kadrey and especially Pat Murphy, from whom I borrowed a name, a typewriter, and some of the plot.

André Breton, Louis Aragon, Jacques Rigaut, Antonin Artaud, Yves Tanguy, and Paul Eluard were real people. All the other characters are probably fictional.

This book is dedicated to my brother Larry, and to Groucho's brother Harpo.

ONE

"Putting life in the service of the unconscious."

Maurice Nadeau,
THE HISTORY OF SURREALISM

The flea market in Saint-Ouen: war medals, glass taxidermists' eyes, a bicycle wheel, a leopard's skin, a pack of cards, an acrobat's costume (for Hélène?) with half the pink sequins gone. Up ahead André Breton and Louis Aragon were arguing animatedly: a short decisive exclamation mark and a cool tall question mark. André was waving his heavy, knobbed cane. Robert St. Onge hung back, watching them from a distance. A phonograph player. Were there recordings too? Aha. There were.

Around him women pushed their babies in prams and haggled over the price of chairs. A boy tripped over the pavement and fell, screaming. A man—he'd seen that man before—walked by singing an obscene song in a foreign accent. Robert picked up records at random, unconcerned, looking for American blues. A photograph fell out onto the table and he turned it over. A dark-haired woman stared back at him. He was looking into the mirror of his desires. Who was she? She was beautiful.

Louis walked past carrying a naked mannequin as tall as himself. "We're leaving soon," he said. "He—" he jerked his head toward André, his hands bound by the mannequin—"says we're meeting back at the café."

"All right," Robert said, putting the photograph back inside the record cover. "I'll get this first." He turned to the woman behind the table—short, fat, almost completely covered by a molting blue feather boa—and discussed the price with her for a few minutes. He noticed for the first time the name of the record, in English, "The Moon's Bright Falling Towers." It didn't look like blues.

André was sitting at a table a few feet away, having his palm read. Robert walked over to him, holding the record carefully. André looked up, troubled. "She says I'm going to be disappointed," he said. "Disappointed by a friend."

"One of us will betray you," Robert said, reminded of André's constant demands for loyalty.

"Disappointed by a friend," the fortune-teller said in a broad country accent. "See? The line says so, here. And maybe disappointed in love too."

"I don't believe you," Robert said. "Who would disappoint you? And how?"

"What do you mean?" André said. To the fortune-teller he said, "We've never met each other before, isn't that true?"

"That's right," she said.

"There, you see?" André said, as if that proved everything. "Objective chance. The moment traps us together, just the two of us. And in the flea market, the unconscious mind of Paris."

"I don't believe it," Robert said again.

"Objective chance," the fortune-teller said. It was obvious from the way she spoke she didn't understand the words. "He's right. You'll see."

"See what?" Robert said. "Are you going to put a curse on me?"

"Unbelievers," the woman said scornfully. "I think that some day we will all go on strike."

"You will?" André said. His somber mood of a moment ago was gone. "For what? For higher wages?" He put his hand in his pocket and drew out a few coins. We'll eat lightly tonight, Robert thought as André gave her a few francs.

"For belief," the woman said. "For magic."

"For dreams," André said seriously. "Go on strike for your dreams."

"For desires," Robert said. He fished in his pocket and drew out his last cigarette. Uncomfortably he wondered if he would be the one to disappoint his friend. He was beginning to find André's obsession with the unconscious tiresome.

"Here," the woman said, standing up and walking slowly around the table. She was a head shorter than he was. "Look. I'll read your palm too. To show you. I'll read it free if you like."

Robert shrugged. André was watching him eagerly, blue-green eyes glittering. Robert switched the record to his other hand and held out his palm.

The woman gasped. "Look at this!" she said. "I've never—Holy God. Look at these lines!"

"What is it?" Robert said, interested in spite of himself. "What do you see?"

"You will go on a long journey," she said.

"That's it?" Robert said. He thought of their old friend Paul Eluard, who had withdrawn money from his father's construction business and was now sending them letters from Polynesia. To be free, to be away from Paris and André's intrigues and this seemingly eternal childhood . . . of course, someday, but still he didn't see why the old woman should be making such a fuss.

"You will travel farther than anyone," she said. "You will—I can't make out this line right here—you will go on a journey of surpassing strangeness. Passion and violence and secrets and death . . ."

"Where?" Robert said, trying to laugh. André was looking at him darkly, eyes hooded. Was he jealous? "To the moon? The stars?"

"No, to Paris. . . ."

André laughed suddenly, a short sardonic laugh. "No, I see what she means," Robert said, strangely moved. "There is nothing on earth more foreign than Paris. Sometimes, in the right light or the right neighborhoods, you can swear you've never seen her before."

"I'm sorry," the woman said. "I didn't mean—I truly don't know what I meant by that. Have you ever had your palm read before?"

"Me?" said Robert. "No, I haven't."

"A young lady once said he'd come to no good end," Louis said, materializing out of the crowd. "That was right before she threw his shoes at him."

"You must," the woman said, ignoring him. "Have it read by someone young, someone not so easily put out of breath. Have someone explain to you—explain why your palm goes so strangely out of focus when it's looked at."

"All right," said Robert, wondering if he ever really would. "I will."

"Good," the woman said. "Good day."

"Well," André said. "Where did you get that?" he said to Louis, indicating the mannequin. "What are you going to do with it?"

"For the Bureau, I thought," Louis said.

"Of course," said André. His face relaxed, the corners of his mouth turned up slightly. Only Robert and Louis could tell that he was smiling. "Good idea. Let's go."

They set out through the streets of Paris. The sun was setting, touching the roofs and chimney pots, filling the alleyways with uneasy dreams. The day was warm for winter. They ran recklessly through the darkening streets, shouting, dodging, knocking the hats off passersby. With Robert in the lead they passed crowds and kiosks, and ducked in and out of cul-de-sacs, blown like meteors across the sky. Their footsteps echoed loudly through old, forgotten neighborhoods. Robert turned back to shout to André, and fell into an old man slowly making his way up a steep cobbled street.

"Excuse me," Robert said. "Excuse me. I'm looking for Robert St. Onge. Have you seen him, by any chance?"

"I—no," the man said, trying to regain his breath. André looked as serious as ever, but Louis, who had arrived late, hampered by the mannequin, was beginning to smile. "No, I haven't. I'm sorry."

"Quite all right," Robert said. "Sorry to have troubled you."

The man tipped his hat and was gone. "Where on earth are we?" André said, looking around.

5

"Quite simple," Robert said. "Through that alley over there, over a few blocks, around a corner and we'll be at the café. You'll see."

Tired now, they returned to the main street. "See that house?" Robert said. "A woman was murdered in that house just a few months ago, shot by her jealous lover. We read about it in the newspaper, remember?"

André nodded. An old woman on the corner was selling flowers. "Strange juxtapositions," Louis said. "Almost poetry, if you like." He was dragging the mannequin behind him now.

"Don't do that," André said. "Her feet will strike sparks off the cobblestones. Do you want to set all of Paris on fire?"

They turned a corner. Rue Fontaine was ahead of them. They began to run again, turning into Place Blanche and arriving at the Cyrano out of breath. "All right," Robert said loudly, standing in the doorway. His broad face was limned with sweat, his brown hair was blown back behind him. "Everyone switch drinks."

A few people in the dim café looked up. No one answered. "Do you suppose they've all gotten used to us?" André asked.

"Huh," said Louis, dragging the mannequin over to a table and propping it on a chair. "I'd like orange-curaçao, please," he said to the waiter. André and Robert followed him in. "And the same for my friend here."

The waiter paused, his pencil suspended over a pad of paper. He shrugged. "Two orange," he said. "And for you two?"

"Grenadine," Robert said. "I like the color."

André ordered orange-curaçao as well. Outside the street was becoming dim. A few stars shook themselves free of the darkness. The street filled with the emptying crowd of the Cirque Médrano, just a few doors down: showgirls, trapeze artists, clowns. Robert leaned back in his chair, watching them parade through his reflection in the glass. "Look!" he said suddenly. "That woman from the show—I saw a sequin outfit just like that this afternoon at the flea market."

"I wonder if it used to belong to her," Louis said.

"All the coincidences," André said. "If only we understood the hidden meanings of things, every event, every object would be a coincidence of the marvelous."

"You wouldn't have to go to the circus then," Robert said.

"Of course not," Louis said. "Look at that crowd out there, those fat and dim-witted people, senses dulled by what they call daily life. Why don't they stay home? You can find the exotic, the dazzling, in an old pair of shoes."

The dark window inverted suddenly, became a mirror. The cold street outside disappeared and Robert saw himself in the reflection of the glass: broad face, dark hair kept a little longer than was fashionable and brushed back, eyes that looked ready to laugh at any absurdity, eyes a lucid brown, as if a light shone behind them, though you couldn't see that in the window. He sighed. The hair was getting thinner, the time was passing. Someone moved into the field of the window.

"Good day," the man said.

"Jacques Rigaut!" André said. "Have a seat."

The short, dapper man remained standing. He held a newspaper under his arm. "Good day," he said to the waiter. "I will have whatever my friend André is having. No, wait a minute. I'll have what that gentleman over there—against the wall, do you see him?—is having."

"That man there?" the waiter said, turning to see better.

"That's right," Jacques said, sitting next to the mannequin. "Thank you very much." The waiter left. "Another one!" Jacques said when he had gone, holding up a small white button. "Clipped it right off his coat when he turned away from me."

"How many does that make now?" Louis said.

"Thirty-two," Jacques said. "Of course some of them"—he emphasized the words—"are worth more than others. As you gentlemen know, being in the art business yourselves."

Outside, the crowd was dispersing. Prostitutes walked up and down the streets or gathered in groups of twos and threes under streetlamps. What do they talk about when they're by themselves? Robert wondered.

André was about to take offense at the words "art business." "Which one is the most valuable right now?" Louis asked.

"Ah, well, it's hard to say," Jacques said. "The vagaries of the business, gentlemen, you know . . . Right now I'd say buttons taken from the uniforms of cops. One must be very careful not to be caught. Of course, I—" he paused to emphasize the word—"have never been arrested."

"I'm not so sure that's something to be proud of," André said. "All the great men and women of history have been in jail. In jail or in mental institutions. Nietzsche, de Sade . . ."

"I'm just as crazy as they were," Jacques said. "I just don't get caught. And when have you ever been arrested? But I didn't mean to begin an argument. I wanted to show you, gentlemen—" he opened the newspaper—"our advertisement, which came out today."

The waiter brought their drinks. "No, no," Louis said as the waiter set two glasses in front of him. "This one is for my friend here." He set one of the glasses in front of the mannequin. "To Monique, the only woman who has ever been faithful to me." He drank.

Jacques tasted his drink. "What is this?" he said. "It tastes horrible." He took another sip.

André was looking through the newspaper. "Here it is," he said finally. " 'Bureau of Surrealistic Research, 15 Rue de Grenelle. We welcome all bearers of secrets: inventors, madmen, revolutionaries, misfits, dreamers. Relate to us your stories, answer our questions, tell us your dreams, leave your work and play with us. We sow the seeds for the new night-blooming flower. Open 1–5.' " He closed the paper. "All right," he said. "We'll see what kind of a response that gets."

Other people were coming into the café now: artists, writers, hangers-on. More chairs were brought over; another table was added. Two women came to the table, giggling. One of them sat in Louis's lap and ran her fingers through his hair. "Is she your new girlfriend?" the woman asked, looking at the mannequin. "She's very beautiful. But a bit naked, don't you think?" Before Louis could stop her she took off her necklace and bracelet—large paste jewels Louis had gotten her at the flea market a few weeks ago—and put them on the mannequin. "There!" she said. "Doesn't that look better?"

"It still looks naked," someone at the table said maliciously.

"Well, then," the woman said. She put her hand to the first button of her blouse. Louis put his hand on top of hers. She looked into his eyes, disappointed, and kissed him.

The large group around the table had split into several smaller ones. Robert leaned back in his chair again, hearing snatches of conversation around him. "He told me he'd throw me out if I couldn't come up with the rent . . ." ". . . Eskimo tribal fetishes . . ." "I haven't talked to her for years now. . . ." "I told him the alchemists wouldn't recognize a distinction like that . . ." He wondered what he could do with the rest of the evening. Maybe Hélène had gotten off work at the café.

Suddenly he heard André's voice, loud with repressed rage. "Do you know what you're talking about?" André said. Robert and several others looked at him. He was talking to two young men—students, probably— who had come in during the last half hour.

"Well, yes," one of them said nervously. "I think so."

"You *think* so," André said. "You think you know what you're saying when you tell us to compromise with the truth, the only truth worth upholding—"

"I didn't say compromise," the young man said. His companion was silent, immobile. Both of them were transfixed by André's blue-green stare. "I said that the best way to reach the workers—I think that the best way to reach the workers would be on a level they understand. Quite frankly, I don't think many people in the factories today understand what you mean by—by surrealism, for example. If you could write a straightforward narrative, something that shows what life in the factories is all about—I wouldn't say this if I didn't have the greatest admiration for your genius, for your brilliance in expressing yourself . . ."

"Isn't that a little patronizing?" André said, icily. " 'The worker can't understand this.' 'The worker isn't ready for that.' You don't have a great deal of respect for the people whose best interests you claim to represent, do you?"

"I didn't mean—" the student said. "I don't—"

"It is the proletariat whose actions will change the world," André said. The student who spoke was nodding eagerly. The other student was still motionless. "They will be at the forefront of all social change. And we—we are at the forefront of artistic change. Once free of the labor of the factory, the worker will turn to us with a thirst he never knew he had—"

Robert tried to suppress a yawn. He had heard this speech of André's before. Outside the café the streets had grown dark. A group of drunks began to enter the café, changed their minds, and turned back the way they'd come. Robert's chair hit the floor loudly. It couldn't be. The light was too dim—it couldn't be— But it was. He got to his feet and ran for the door, ignoring the students' puzzled stares, André's shout, Louis's quiet smile.

The woman whose face he had seen in the photograph was turning the corner. She was taller than he thought she'd be from her picture. As she passed under the streetlamp her black curly hair glowed with red highlights.

Robert ran after her. The street seemed to elongate as he turned the corner; the houses moved for a moment and then were still. Someone shouted. A loud blasting noise came from the direction of the river. Terrified he ran on, hoping he hadn't lost her. He felt horribly disoriented now. Where was he? "The police!" a high woman's voice said to his right. "The police are coming!"

He blinked, blinked again as his eyes teared from the smoke. Those impossibly tall buildings—surely he would have noticed them before. "Get down!" someone said loudly. He rubbed his eyes, wincing, but the buildings stayed the same.

"Hey, stupid!" the voice said again. "They're coming. Do you want to get shot?"

He looked around. A barricade had been built out of torn-up cobblestones and overturned cars. There was something wrong with the cars, too—they were too small, and there were too many of them. A shot sounded, closer this time. He ran for the barricade and climbed over.

"You certainly took your time about it," the man said. He had round glasses and glossy hair that fitted him like a cap.

"Where am I?" Robert said. "I—I think I'm lost."

The man looked at him strangely. "Lost?" he said. "You shouldn't have come out tonight at all if you don't know your way around. Where have you been the last couple of days?"

"Me?" Robert said. "I've been right here." His hands were sweaty. His heart pounded wildly. "What's going on?"

"It's the revolution, man," the other man said. "The general strike. Get the hell down, would you?" A piece of cobblestone hit the barricade and bounced off harmlessly.

"No . . ." Robert said. How could this be happening? In one rash move he had lost everything—his friends, the cafés, the streets of Paris. "What—where am I? Is this Paris?"

"Of course this is Paris," the other man said. "What are you—crazy?"

"If they've broken into the asylums, the revolution's already gone further than we thought," a woman's voice said. Robert turned to her eagerly, but it was not the woman from his phonograph recording. She had long, straight brown hair and close-set eyes.

"I'm not—I don't think I'm crazy," Robert said,

stalling for time. The revolution. The revolution that André and the others had talked about so many times in the dim cozy cafés. Had they somehow conjured it up? Why weren't they here instead of him? He had never wanted revolution—all he had wanted was to have a good time and be left alone.

A siren sounded in the distance. Suddenly a group of people—kids, really—ran around the corner toward the barricade. Helmeted men followed, some holding guns. A few of the men— Policemen? Robert thought incredulously. Here?—stopped when they saw the barricade, but half a dozen continued on. One shot wildly into the crowd. The rest of the men were falling back. The kids made it to the barricade and leapt over. One of them was left on the ground, his right leg splayed outward at an unnatural angle. Blood had started to seep through the pants. The man who had shot him hesitated a moment, looked quickly at the barricade, and turned and ran. One of the kids picked up a loose paving stone and threw it at the corner, hitting a building. He picked up another one, lighter this time, and tossed it back and forth between his hands.

"We've got to go get him, Paul," the woman was saying. They were all ignoring Robert.

"I don't know if we can risk moving him," Paul said.

"We've got to," the woman said. "I heard them saying over the radio today that the Red Cross isn't coming this far any more. We're all he has."

"We're not much," Paul said. "Who's to say we won't hurt him somehow when we move him?"

"And what if the police get him?" the woman said. "We're better than nothing."

One of the kids cleared his throat. "I know a little

nursing," he said. "Been studying it a little. We need something to move him on."

The woman stood up—Robert was slightly shocked to notice that she was wearing pants—and walked over to one of the cars turned on its side, climbed on top of it and opened the passenger door. "Aha," she said a moment later. "I knew I'd find something." She was holding a warm woolen blanket. "Let's go."

This time Robert stared at her in frank astonishment. Was she about to go out there and risk the police? She and the kid who knew nursing climbed over the paving stones. She still held the blanket. Robert thought of Hélène, soft, slightly plump, waiting at her fashionable Left Bank café for a rich American to take her to the States with him.

A few minutes later they returned with the injured kid on the blanket. Robert looked at him, then looked away. The bone had broken clear through the fabric of the pants. So this is revolution, he thought savagely, imagining André there beside him. I hope you like it.

The kid who knew nursing took out a small knife and cut the pants leg away. "We'll need a fire," he said. "The nights can get pretty cold."

"I don't think that's safe," Paul said. "What if they come back?"

The kid on the blanket moaned softly. "He's coming to," the other kid said.

"They won't be back," the woman said. "You saw the way they ran."

"They could see the light and drop tear gas," Paul said.

"We're just going to have to take that risk," the kid said. He was doing something to the leg Robert couldn't see. The kid on the blanket cried out once and fell back into unconsciousness. "He could die."

"Goddamn it," Paul said. He sounded angry now. "I thought I was the leader here. How are we ever going to get anything done if no one's in charge?"

The woman looked at him, silent for a moment. Finally she said, "That's what we're trying to find out, Paul." Robert had the feeling that they were picking up the thread of an old argument. "That's what we're fighting for. A world without leaders."

Paul looked around for support. "All right," he said. "All right. Take a vote or whatever it is you do. Meanwhile the kid will probably die from lack of attention and the police will be just delighted at our bickering, but go ahead. I won't try to help out again."

They did seem to be taking a vote. Finally a few of them began breaking branches off the trees behind the barricade. Robert saw someone in one of the buildings flick a curtain at the window, look out, and then disappear back into the apartment.

"Matches," someone said. "Anyone got matches?"

Robert took the box of matches from his pocket and threw it to him. The fear rose up within him again. Just this afternoon, standing peacefully in the flea market, he had lit his last cigarette from that box of matches. Another link with his world gone. Strange juxtapositions, Louis had said, also just this afternoon. Was this poetry? Louis would probably say it was. Robert thought it was too bloody to be poetry.

They had gotten the fire going. The kid who had been shot still lay unconscious. Robert watched as the fire climbed the ladders of branches, destroying as it went. He felt desolate, stranded without friends. No. He had to leave, had to keep moving. "Anyone see a tall woman, dark hair, your age or a little older?" he said, trying to keep his voice light. "I think she passed this way tonight."

A few of the kids looked at each other and shrugged. Paul stirred from beside the fire. "No," he said. "I don't think so." Robert thought that there was something Paul wasn't saying. Did Paul think he was a cop? "Though I could have missed her with everything else going on." He fed a small branch to the fire.

"Thanks," Robert said. He stood up.

"Where are you going?" the woman asked. "You're not leaving?"

"I have to," Robert said. "I have to find her." Or get back to where I came from, he thought.

"It's dangerous out there," Paul said. "They've been spraying us with tear gas all night."

Was tear gas anything like the gas in the trenches? The thought frightened him, but he knew he had to go. "Good night," he said, heading for the barricade and climbing over.

Fear and excitement hit him as he turned the corner. The buildings around the corner were still unfamiliar, taller, shinier, their glass windows larger. Now what? he thought, the excitement turning in a moment to despair. How was he to get back? He had once known Paris as well as he knew his own body. What was he to do in this strange bloody place, changed out of all recollection like something from a half-remembered nightmare?

He turned down a street at random. Perhaps he could still get to some landmark, the Eiffel Tower or Notre Dame. His footsteps were slow and uncertain, a dreamer's walk. A shot sounded in the distance and a burst of shots answered. Bright colors lit the sky, smeared and ran to the ground. Fireworks, he thought tiredly. They were fighting with fireworks.

Up ahead a woman walked by herself. The fireworks flowered against the sky. Her hair reflected the lights, red, blue, green, the colors of a crown. He ran after her, no longer tired. "Wait," he said. "Who are you? Where—?"

She turned, a look of recognition on her face. Had she been searching for him too then? "Quick!" she said. Her voice was low and powerful. "We have to tell you—" She looked angered, resigned, hopeful all in the space of a moment. Fireworks scattered around them, fragments of color like the snows of strange lands. He stood watching the mobility of her face, the beauty of it. "The avenues of time are closing," she said. "Quick! Remember—" she paused for a bare second, considering—"remember that your imagination is real. Forget everything else."

"I don't—I don't understand," he said. She was becoming smaller, leaving him, though she hadn't moved. "Wait!" he said. "Please—please tell me—"

"I'll try to see you again," she said. She grew smaller and smaller in the space of an eyeblink. "No, don't," he said, feeling lost. The buildings around him wavered and grew faint, and were replaced by smaller buildings, houses and apartments of his time. The woman disappeared.

After a moment's confusion he knew where he was. To his right, about three blocks over, was the river. The smell of gunpowder was gone, replaced by the tang of salt and seawater. There was his apartment and Café Cyrano over that way, in Montmartre. Hélène was across the river. Where should he go? Nowhere. He did not want to talk to anyone. It was late in the night.

Paris turned under the stars. The wind whistled past cafés and opera houses, past the rich and the poor. The dead slept, men and women walked slowly together, bound for their own mysterious arrivals. Leaves fell softly to the gutters.

Robert picked a direction and started walking aimlessly. He put his hands in his pockets, unconsciously searching for a cigarette. Who was that woman? What was she doing, where was she going? She set his imagination going as it had not been for a long time. He could think up wild explanations and possibilities for her presence, give her half a dozen strange pasts, all of which he believed. Was it her mystery that fascinated him, or her beauty? Or was it what she had said to him, words that seemed to answer questions he hadn't remembered asking? She had said that she would try to see him again. But when?

He laughed as a thought came to him. For years André had talked of the ideal of passionate love, of the one woman of a man's lifetime who helps him understand everything. It had become something of a joke between him and a few of the others. Every affair, every woman casually taken home for the night, had been explained to André as the one true love. Robert had laughed about it—cruelly, he saw now—with Hélène after she had told him her fantasies about the rich American. And now it had happened to him. The passionate ideal. And he could never tell anyone.

He walked toward the lights of the Tuileries Gardens, passing quietly through the trees. How could he tell André, after all? He had known André since— He stopped a minute. Since 1917, that awful and miraculous year, the year he had gotten trench fever and been sent home from the front. André, a medical student then, had been working in a mental hospital. They had met in a bookstore, reaching for the same volume of Rimbaud.

Seven years. André had intrigued him at first, telling him stories about the patient who hadn't believed in the reality of the war, had stood up on the trenches and not been shot. Another patient had changed his name and style of clothing from day to day in an effort to stave off boredom. Robert and André had talked endlessly about the futility of war, the necessity of changing life, of breaking free . . . And then Louis had joined them (Where had Louis come from? It was like trying to remember the plot of a novel long after you'd finished it.) and somehow, by means Robert still did not understand, they had gathered followers and become a major literary and artistic movement.

And André still intrigued him. The passionate debates, the scandalized looks on the faces of the bourgeoisie when together they interrupted a literary dinner or tore apart a theatrical opening . . . André was alive. Too many of the friends of his youth were dead, shot in the trenches or killed by the fever, and too many of them were moving toward a kind of living death, encased in jobs, families, houses, servants. Never work, André had said, and Robert had followed that advice as much as he could, living on a small allowance from his family and taking part-time jobs proofreading when he had to.

But it was time to move on. Seven years of anything was enough. André took himself seriously now, talking about dialectical materialism and the unconscious and objective chance . . . What was wrong with just having a good time? When had everyone gotten so serious? And then there was the novel he wanted to write, the novel about Paris that would have nothing to do with surrealism at all. André would disapprove and that would be it: he'd be excommunicated, thrown out of the movement.

So he couldn't tell André about the woman. It would be reinterpreted to fit in with surrealist canon. Passionate love, trance states, the unconscious mind—he

19

could hear André's speech now. And that would be ridiculous, when the woman hadn't been about any of those things at all, when she had been—

He stopped a moment, looked around. Up ahead he could see the Sacre-Coeur Basilica. Montmartre, André, and the café were straight ahead. He turned left down a side street, knowing he wouldn't get lost.

When she was what? he asked himself, realizing that he'd been thinking about the past, about the known, to avoid having to think about the woman and the unknown. Where had she taken him? To the future, perhaps. Or to the past, the Paris Commune or the Revolution. No, that couldn't be right, because of the cars. Was he going crazy? What would André think if he were?

It had been Paris, though a cold, changed, almost soulless Paris. He was sure of that. For the first time he thought of the fortune-teller at the flea market. "Passion and violence and secrets and death." He drew his coat closer around him, feeling the cold winter wind. What had he blundered into? All right then, he thought. No more chasing after strange women. But even as he thought it, he didn't believe it. The adventure had to be followed to the end.

Who was she? he thought again. Why did the world he knew waver and shift around her? He hadn't even looked at her name on the phonograph recording. The recording, he thought, suddenly panicked. It was back at the café. He began to run.

Two old men sat at a table by the window, watching him without curiosity as he came in. Another man swept the floor with unhurried strokes. Robert ran to the table he had shared with André and the others. The record was gone.

"Excuse me," he said to the man sweeping the

floor. "Did you see a phonograph record on the floor near this table?"

"A phonograph record?" the man said slowly. "Why, no, sir."

"Are you sure?" Robert asked.

"Of course I'm sure," the man said. "That was the table with the mannequin, right, sir? And later someone wanted to take all the ashtrays home."

Robert shrugged. That sounded right. "Listen," he said, trying not to sound too urgent. "If you do find it, would you tell me? I come here all the time. I can give you a reward."

The man's eyes brightened at the mention of the reward. "They certainly were a strange group of people," he said. "I don't know why they bothered to come here—they should have been across the river with the students and the tourists and the rest of them."

Robert shrugged again. He was not about to explain André's dislike of the Left Bank crowd to this man. "Remember what I said," he said. "About the reward."

"I will," the man said.

"Good night."

Robert left the café and went out into the deserted street. It was very late—the moon had set. He yawned. He had eaten no dinner. He could hunt up the rest of the crowd—probably at André's house on Rue Fontaine—or he could go to his apartment and go to sleep. He yawned again and set out for home.

TWO

"The visitors, born under a remote star or next door, helped elaborate this formidable machine for killing what is in order to fulfill what is not. At number 15, Rue de Grenelle, we opened a romantic Inn for unclassifiable ideas and continuing revolts. All that still remained of hope in this despairing universe would turn its last, raving glances toward our pathetic stall. It was a question of formulating a new declaration of the rights of man."

Louis Aragon

Robert woke late the next day. Weak winter light the color of cider shone through the uncurtained windows. He turned in bed and looked at the clock on the nightstand—a quarter to one—then lay back, rubbing his eyes. The clock had stopped sometime last week. He stretched and sat up.

Last night's clothes were jumbled together in a pile on the floor. He picked up his coat carefully: it smelled of gunpowder and machine oil and something he couldn't identify. A cold stab of fear went through him. It had been real, then. For a minute he thought he had dreamed it.

He could see himself as he was last night, sharp and distant as a figure in a motion picture. There he was jumping over the barricade, startling at gunfire. There he was wandering the streets alone. These things don't happen, he thought. They don't. He felt alone again, bereft. Whom could he tell? Suppose it happened again? He threw last night's clothes into a corner, dressed and went downstairs.

"Good afternoon, sir," the concierge said.

"Uh—good afternoon," Robert said. "Do you know— What time is it?"

"You came in late again last night, didn't you?" the woman said. "I heard you and woke up. It's near two now—I guess you got about a full night's sleep. You think you'll ever make your parents happy and get a regular job?"

Robert smiled weakly. "No," he said, stepping out into the street.

In the afternoon the events of last night seemed unreal. He had pushed back the doors of a movie theatre and stepped into daylight. The feeling of desolation that had welled over him earlier was gone. His friends were waiting for him, about to begin the day's games.

Where to first? he thought. Food, of course. He was suddenly ravenous. Breakfast somewhere, and another box of cigarettes, and then— Where did André say they were meeting today? Right. The Bureau of Surrealistic Research, across the river.

An hour or so later he was walking down Rue de Grenelle. A pleasant thought had come to him at breakfast: maybe André or one of the others had taken the record home last night for safekeeping. He whistled a little to himself, looking down the street for a landmark.

Ahead of him a young man he didn't know stood on the sidewalk. Robert slowed, recognizing the Bureau. "Good afternoon," the young man said. He held out his fist, palm down, and without thinking Robert put his own hand underneath it. The young man, smiling mysteriously, dropped something into Robert's hand. Robert looked. It was a dog whistle.

"Good afternoon," the young man said again to a well-dressed businessman behind Robert, handing him an English penny. He gave the next person a flat balloon. A woman wrapped in furs got a small dead fish.

Robert went inside. Louis was standing on a ladder in the middle of the room, trying to hang the mannequin from the ceiling. It still wore the paste jewels from the night before. A book was fastened to the wall with forks. "Good afternoon," André said, turning away from a window he had been trying unsuccessfully to open. "You're late."

"I overslept," Robert said. He didn't remember André's mentioning a specific time to meet. "My clock stopped." He took out a cigarette and lit it.

"Mmmm," André said. "I think you and Antonin will stay here today. I have to get the magazine to the printers. Tomorrow—maybe Yves and someone else. I don't know. I haven't got the whole thing figured out yet."

"You think so," Robert said, annoyed. He hadn't fully realized it until that moment, but a part of him had planned to walk the streets of Paris until evening. Perhaps the woman would reappear. "Don't you think you should have asked me first?"

"I did ask you," André said. "When we first came

up with the idea. You said of course you'd be willing to work with us."

"I didn't say I'd be willing to work today," Robert said. "As it happens I'm busy. And anyway whatever happened to your idea of never working? You don't expect me to sit in an office every day taking messages, do you?"

"Don't be ridiculous," André said.

"I'll be ridiculous if I want to," Robert said hotly, but his friend cut him off. "You know what this means to us, to our movement," André said. "We've discussed this. It's important work, work that needs to be done. You remember when we did the dream research."

"Yes, well, I'm doing my own research today," Robert said. "Sorry. Maybe some other time."

André blinked. "What are you doing?" he said.

Robert hesitated. He stood on the brink of telling him. They had been so close to each other at one time. But André would only ridicule him, denigrate his interests. He said nothing.

"Where did you go last night?" André asked. "We had an excellent session back at my house— I managed to put three or four people into trances. Some interesting things—you should have been there."

"I— I had to meet a woman," Robert said.

"Hélène?" André said.

"No," Robert said, unwilling to say more.

"What's her name?" André said.

Robert hesitated. They faced each other across a chasm of years. Something in André's face made Robert wonder if he too were thinking of when there had been just the two of them. "I don't know," he said finally. "I'm looking for her again today. I think that maybe she bears my fate."

Surprisingly André nodded. "All right," he said.

25

"Feelings that strong can't be denied. I'll get someone else to work today."

"Thanks," Robert said. "Oh—one more thing. Did you see a phonograph record last night at the café? I left it there by accident."

"A phonograph record?" André said, shaking his head. "Are you sure? There are no accidents." And he turned back to the window.

Robert left the Bureau uncertain of what to do next. His desire to be with his friends had turned into a desire to find the woman, to follow her to his strange destiny. He walked restlessly past restaurants, court-yards, railroad tracks, bridges. The woman did not come back. The woman would never come back again. He would be free to pursue his own life without the uncertainty that shook him whenever he saw a head of curly black hair. Why didn't he feel relieved?

The sun was writing long shadows on the pavement when he stopped. Tourists thronged the Boulevard: he heard the flat drawl of American accents. Hélène's café was just a few blocks over. Why not? he thought. Why not settle back into a life of prosaic routine? He jostled past the bicycles and people and continued down the street.

Hélène was waiting behind the bar, joking with a customer. Her hair was piled up on top of her head, her eyes darkened by mascara. She laughed. Somehow he was always surprised to see how genuine her laugh was, surrounded by all that false glamour. Her teeth were crooked, and he was always surprised to see that too.

"Hello," he said, coming in.

"Well hello!" she said warmly, stepping out from behind the bar. Her breasts were pushed up and out by her skimpy costume. As usual he felt both annoyed and excited by her outfit. "What have you been up to?"

"Oh, you know," he said. "Not much."

"Where were you last night?" she said.

"Out with André and the rest of them," he said, not wanting to tell her more. "The usual thing."

"Usual!" she said, laughing. She had never understood André's theories and he had given up trying to explain them to her. "Sitting in a café until all hours, talking, God knows what . . . Is André still trying to hypnotize people?"

Robert nodded. "He did it again last night," he said.

"He did?" she said. "Did he try to hypnotize you too?" She had always distrusted André a little.

"No," Robert said. "I didn't want him to." He felt uncomfortable lying. As far as he could remember he had never lied to her.

"And what else?" she said, still smiling. "Poetry, strange incantations, mumbo jumbo? You do lead a strange life, Robert."

"Strange?" Robert said. "I was just thinking how routine it was. Up every day at two—"

Hélène laughed. Robert stopped. He hadn't meant to be funny. "I'm sorry," she said, muffling her laughter with her hand. "Go on."

"Up every day, over to the cafés, to André's, to sleep at about four in the morning . . . I don't know. They're interesting people, but somehow. . . ."

"You're crazy, you know that?" Hélène said. "Do you know how many people dream of living your life? You said André told you and all the others never to work and that's the only thing he's ever said that's made any sense to me. Do you know how much I want to stop working?" Robert looked at her, surprised. She had never been this serious with him before. "I had to start working when I was fourteen," she said. "My parents came to the city from the country—all right, they were ignorant, they thought there might be a better life here. And there wasn't, and there wasn't any food to be had like there might have been on the farms, and so I had to start working. I had to pretend I was older, had to develop a Parisian accent . . . You laugh at me because I want to marry a rich American, and— and all right, I laugh too, but it's my one chance. It's my one chance to live like you do. You're living. I'm just surviving."

She had never talked about her parents before. Somehow Robert had always thought she had been born in Paris. "Listen," she said, a little embarrassed. "Stop by more often. We never get a chance to be together any more—you're always with that crowd. I miss you."

"All right," Robert said, feeling obscurely guilty, feeling pulled in too many directions at once. "I will. After I spend some time at the café. I'll stop by when you get off work."

"Good," she said, smiling. "See you."

" 'Bye," Robert said.

He retraced his steps back to the Bureau. It had been stupid to think that the woman would return. She had come into his life for a night of smoke and blood and had left again, like a dream. Maybe he would tell André about her when the group had another dream session. He could never remember his dreams anyway.

Antonin Artaud waited for him at the entrance to the Bureau. "I knew you'd be back," he said. "I've been waiting for you." He leaned against the doorjamb, blocking the entrance with his body.

"Not just me, I hope," Robert said. Antonin made

him a little uncomfortable. He wondered where André's obsession with madmen would finally lead.

"Of course not," Antonin said. "All the world will pass through this doorway. First the shamans, the magicians. The Dalai Lama. The Dalai Lama might have passed through today—if he did you missed him. And then everyone. Everyone is a magician. Everyone is the Dalai Lama."

"Everyone?" Robert said. "Even me?"

"Even you," Antonin said. "It's hard to tell. Things were a lot clearer inside the asylum. I would have known who you were then."

"I'm Robert," he said easily. "I was supposed to work with you today. Did anyone interesting come by? Anything happen?"

"A parade of elephants came thundering down the street, each one holding a sapphire in his trunk. A striped balloon landed on the roof. You think I'm crazy, don't you?" Antonin watched Robert shrewdly, his eyes glinting. "What if I told you this was all metaphor? Surrealist metaphor? André would understand—André is a true magus. As you are not. You laugh at us—you think we're amusing."

"That's right," Robert said, wondering what André would think of this conversation. He and André could never be this candid. "I just want to have a good time."

"A good time," Antonin said. "There's a dead place in your soul."

"Well, what happened today?" Robert said. The direction of the conversation was making him uneasy. "Did anyone come in?"

"Oh yes," Antonin said. "A child came by, looking for her mother. A man wanted to tell us his dream about bees. A woman was looking for her hairdresser,

29

one block over. And a man stopped by with a phonograph record. He said it was for you."

"For me?" Robert said. His heart began to pound loudly, almost drowning out Antonin's words. "What—what kind of phonograph record?"

"For you," Antonin said again. "That's why I was waiting for you."

"Well, where is it?" Robert asked. He made a move toward the doorway. Antonin stayed where he was.

"Not so fast," Antonin said. "First you have to promise to work tomorrow. It will be good for your soul."

"All right," Robert said. Antonin moved away from the doorway and went inside. Robert followed him. The mannequin and the book were still there. A desk stood by the window, which was still closed. Everything else was the same. Antonin reached behind the desk and brought out the record, the same one Robert had bought at the flea market. Robert glanced at it quickly. Solange. The woman's name was Solange. He held the record close to him.

"You're sure a man brought this in?" Robert said. "Not a woman?"

Antonin looked at him witheringly. "I may be crazy," he said finally. "I'm not stupid."

"I just wondered," Robert said. "What did he look like?"

"Like a man," Antonin said, shrugging. "He had a strange accent. Maybe he was the Dalai Lama."

"All right," Robert said, exasperated. "You're not amusing any more. If I were the leader of this band of lunatics instead of André I'd have you excommunicated. Thrown out for not being amusing enough."

"Do you see this?" Antonin said, pointing to the

book attached to the wall. Robert blinked at the sudden change of subject. "Do you know what it is?"

Robert shook his head.

"Fantômas," Antonin said. Robert shrugged. André and a few of the others were interested in the adventures of the pulp character, but Robert had never read any of the books. "It's about Fantômas. You know who he is, don't you? He's the master thief. He slips past locks and guards and scales high walls, and all the time you swear your house is completely safe he's taking the jewels you stored last winter in the basement. That's the man who brought you your record. He steals the thing most precious to you."

Antonin was speaking quickly now, his eyes never leaving Robert's. Perhaps he had taken seriously Robert's demand that he be more amusing. "If he takes the thing that's most precious," Robert said, "why did he bother to bring it back?"

"That's the way a master thief works," Antonin said. "He makes you think you're safe, but you're not. Your most precious possession is still missing."

"And what's that?" Robert asked.

"Your heart," Antonin said. "The woman stole your heart. The woman you're waiting for, the one you thought brought the record back." And he laughed loudly.

"All right," Robert said again. He didn't want to admit to Antonin how accurate he had been. "I'm going back to the café."

"Wait a minute," Antonin said. "It's way past five. I'll go with you." He took a ring of keys from his pocket and locked the door behind him. Robert wondered why André had entrusted Antonin with the keys. "Keys," Antonin said, as though reading his mind, "to the Theatre of Dreams."

They set out through the darkening city together.

31

Antonin walked silently beside Robert, smoking cigarettes rapidly as though burning off ideas and fantasies. The glow of the cigarettes flickered in front of him in unreadable cipher. Robert was glad not to have to talk to him. He lit one of his cigarettes and tossed the match into the Seine as they crossed over. Bells tolled out over the silent city—six o'clock, or was it seven? He had lost count somewhere in the middle.

As they walked through the streets of Montmartre he remembered again the events of the night before. His heart pounded, he held on to the record more tightly as they turned the corner that had been the entryway into that strange night. Nothing happened. He was still in the Paris he knew. He loosened his grip on the record.

He and Antonin paused in the doorway to the café. The warm weather had held through the day, but the night was chilly. André, Louis and some of the others sat at the same table, beckoning to them. They entered and brought a few more chairs over to the table. Robert sat facing the window. The waiter came and took their order.

"How did it go?" André asked. "What went on at the Bureau today?"

Antonin told him. Robert leaned back in his chair, staring out at the dim streets beyond the window. The lights of the city were coming on one by one. Would she return tonight?

"A phonograph record?" André said. "The record you were looking for this afternoon?"

Robert looked away from the window reluctantly. "That's right," he said.

"Is that it?" André said.

Robert nodded. He handed the recording to André, taking it back before André was quite through looking at it. "He brought that in specifically for you?" André asked. Robert nodded again. "How did he know you'd be there?"

"You explain it to me," Robert said. "You're the one who's always talking about coincidences."

"A ruthless coincidence," André said. "A marvelous coincidence. You think you understand your life, and then the unconscious emerges and capsizes your mind."

"Yes, but explain it to me," Robert said impatiently. André might talk about the marvelous all he wanted but Robert seemed to be drowning in it. He wanted answers. "Who was he, where did he get the record, how did he know where to deliver it?"

"You can't ask questions like that," André said. "The unconscious has its own logic." But he looked a little puzzled, a little too tied to the world of logic and order.

The waiter brought their drinks and Robert took a sip from his. He felt as though he were surrounded by children. "You did quite well," André said to Antonin. "We've only been open one day and the world of Paris begins to sift through our hands."

"He found the record in the café last night and then asked someone who I was," Robert said, interrupting. "We're not exactly inconspicuous. Or maybe Antonin made the whole thing up. You see—you can ask questions like that. You can answer them, too."

"There's a dead place in your soul," Antonin said. He emptied his glass in three swallows and dropped the glass to the floor. Clear crystal rang out as it shattered. A few of the patrons looked around. Some of them laughed nervously and returned to their drinks. "An alarm clock," Antonin said. "An alarm clock to wake you up. It's a poem."

The waiter came hurrying from the back of the café. "What happened?" he asked. "We'll have to charge you for the glass."

"What do you mean?" Antonin said. "I should charge you for the poem."

"All right," Louis said quickly. "We'll pay for the glass."

The waiter wrote something on his pad. "Thank you, sir," he said. He nodded and left.

"You're too conciliatory, Louis," Antonin said. He picked up another drink, downed it and held the glass over the floor. "Should I drop it? Or not? What do you think? To drop it? Or not?"

"I don't think so, Antonin," Louis said. His hand was nervously poised to catch the glass if it fell.

"No," Antonin said. He set the glass back on the table. "The first one was enough. I just wanted to wake up Robert."

"I still feel a little sleepy," Robert said. The way to deal with Antonin, he knew, was never to let him see you were afraid.

"That's your own problem," Antonin said. "Whose drink was this? Tomorrow maybe we'll wake you up a bit more. At the Bureau."

"You're working at the Bureau tomorrow, Robert?" André said.

Robert nodded, straining to see beyond his reflection in the window. "I promised I would." The prospect of a day at the Bureau no longer seemed dull. Perhaps the man who had brought in the record would return.

"Good," André said. Robert could tell he was pleased. "I'm glad you're with us. You'll see how important the work is."

"No work is important, if you ask me," Robert said, but André did not hear him.

The talk around the table fragmented again. Louis was talking about a company he had heard of that would post unstamped letters from anywhere in the world. "Think of it," he said. "Your friends would think you were on a grand cruise in the far east, and you could be—anywhere. You could be in Paris." Someone wondered where Paul Eluard was then— "Maybe he's outside, waiting for us. Maybe he's there now." André brought out the latest postcard from Polynesia, full of scrawls and exclamation marks. Yves Tanguy began to tell a story about a man who claimed that he was employed to live someone else's life. "His employer was too frightened to go out and do anything by himself, so he hired this man to live for him. He'd go to bars and get into fights, went climbing in the Himalayas, became a smuggler in Africa, took monk's vows for about a month . . . And everywhere he went he'd bring back something, some souvenir, so that the employer could claim to have done these things himself. Or that's what he told me, anyway."

"Sounds like a wonderful job," Louis said. "Where do I apply?"

"He was leaving when I talked to him," Yves said. "Something about coral fishing in the Pacific."

"Listen," André said. "*La Révolution Surréaliste* is going to the printer's tomorrow. Write that down and we'll publish it."

"Write it down?" Yves said. He laughed. "It's just an amusing story. I'll write it if I remember."

"We need poems, too," André said. His seriousness infected the group. "You, Robert, you haven't given us anything in a long time."

"A poem?" Robert said. "All right. Do you want automatic writing? Give me a pencil."

André found him a pencil. Robert lit a cigarette

and drew on it thoughtfully for a moment. The sounds of conversation, of clinking glasses, of the waiters calling to one another faded into the background. Everything was blank, drawn up into the white spiral of the cigarette smoke. He pulled a napkin over and began to write:

"It is morning, and the sun comes up with the vibrant urgency of a line of mustachioed men.

It is morning, and the telephone rings in the next room like a waterfall sounding in the forest.

The dark-haired woman says good-bye at the station . . ."

André wouldn't approve of the line about the dark-haired woman. You weren't supposed to make references to anything in the real world. Still, André didn't have to know.

He handed the finished poem to André. "Good," André said, putting the napkin in his pocket. "Anyone else?"

"If your friend were here he'd want to take the napkin home with him," someone said to Yves. "So his employer could claim to have been a surrealist."

"I think I might have something for the magazine," Louis said. "I'd like to read it aloud first, though."

"All right," André said. "Let's go to my place for the reading. Or should we have dinner first?"

Robert looked out the window anxiously. It was late, later than it had been when the woman had made her appearance yesterday. She probably won't come today, he thought. Or she had come already and he had missed her. He glanced at the record on the floor, making sure that it was still there.

"I—I think I'll be going," Robert said. "I promised someone I'd meet her tonight."

"Who?" André said. "The woman you were telling me about?"

"No," Robert said. He tried to meet André's eyes and failed. "Hélène."

André looked disappointed. "Passionate love is the love of only one woman," he said finally.

Robert shrugged, uncomfortable. "I'm very fond of her," he said. "Of Hélène."

"All right," André said unhappily. Clearly he had decided not to argue this once. "See you tomorrow."

" 'Bye," Robert said. He picked up the record and went outside.

Rain had washed the street down, making it shine like a ribbon. Light from the cafés spangled against the pavement. Muffled cars drove by, illuminating raindrops like needles, but the street was empty of people. The night was too cold for walking. He buttoned his coat against the chill and counted the money in his pocket. Ten days till the end of the month and the next check from his parents. So much for food, for rent, for objects found in flea markets. He stood caught in the web of a delicate algebra, pulled one way then another by the weight of his desires. Finally he shrugged and headed for the Métro station across the street. By the end of the month he would be walking everywhere.

He got out near the cafés on the Left Bank. Garish lights abolished the night, the clouds. Loud jazz came from the Coupole. He stopped in, had a drink with a few of the musicians and ended up going out to dinner with them. At the Dôme down the street he had another drink and sat awhile listening to Kiki sing. No one he knew came in and he left at around two to pick up Hélène.

They took the Métro back to his apartment. The cold had seeped into the apartment and the gas heater he had bought at a flea market had been broken since some time last spring. "Is that the time?" Hélène said, looking at the clock. "I thought it was later than that."

"It is," Robert said, leading her to the bed. There was only one chair in the apartment. "The clock stopped."

"It did?" Hélène said. "When?"

"A quarter to one," Robert said, distracted, beginning to kiss her. They made love with most of their clothes on. Afterwards Hélène went down the hall to wash her makeup off and came back to sit on the bed. Robert watched as she settled back, arranging the blankets over her. Sometimes she seemed almost not to know what a beautiful body she had. "How are things?" she asked. "What did you do today?" She yawned; perhaps the question was just meant to be polite.

"Nothing much," Robert said. "Wandered around . . . André wants me to work on this new project of his tomorrow—the Bureau of Surrealistic Research."

"Do you want to?"

"I don't know," he said, noticing for the first time how much genuine interest was in her questions, how her questions always seemed to elicit long answers from him. Maybe he should ask her how she was, ask about her day. But he felt uncomfortable. He had been drawn to her at first by her joking references to her rich American—he had known then that there wouldn't be any talk of marriage between them. But did he want to get closer? Did she? "I think I might. It's just that André—I don't see why he feels he can give me orders. There's always some project of his—something he has to do—"

"And you can't just refuse?" Hélène said. Robert had a brief fantasy of her in wire-rimmed glasses, Dr. Freud's young assistant. He had seen Freud a few years after the war, at a lecture André had taken him to. She had missed her calling.

"I don't want to refuse," he said. "They're interesting—that's the trouble. Everything André thinks of is interesting. I'll probably be there tomorrow." He couldn't tell her about the phonograph recording. "But—I don't know—someday—maybe I will refuse."

"I don't really understand why you've stayed with him this long," Hélène said. "Seven years?"

Robert sighed. "I don't either," he said. "Did I ever tell you about the day I knew André was my friend?"

Hélène shook her head.

"Someone I'd been with at the front had come to visit me," Robert said. "My mother had given him my address. I don't know why—maybe she thought he'd be a good influence on me. I was drifting, thinking not very seriously about going into medicine . . . Anyway his leg had been shot off. He was very loud coming into my room—I didn't live on Rue Caroline then, I was on the ground floor—and he sat down and started to talk about the war. I couldn't hear him—I kept wondering why his leg had been shot off and I still had both of mine. We'd both had the same chances, you know."

Hélène nodded. Robert moved next to her and pulled the blankets over them both. "But after a while," he said, "after a while—well, it seemed as though he didn't even notice his leg was gone. As though he didn't notice that anything was changed, that everything was changed, that the war had changed everything. He kept talking about how we'd beaten back the enemy, and the world was safe again, and how he was back as manager of some glassworks and about the woman he was probably going to marry . . . And he wanted to talk about the war, and how much fun it was to crawl through mud and dead bodies and advance perhaps as much as ten feet, and then wait for hours until it was time to crawl again. And I wondered, well, maybe he didn't just have his leg missing, maybe he was dead. Maybe there was a ghost sitting in my kitchen, speaking dead ideas. Because how could someone have lived through the war, lived through all that, and still believe what he believed?" He paused. Hélène said nothing. "I thought everything was going to be different," he said. "I had changed—I thought everyone else had too."

"We had," Hélène said. "Maybe not enough. We just wanted life to go on."

"I did too," Robert said. "But a different kind of life—a real life. I thought everyone could see how they'd lied to us about the war, how they'd probably lied about everything else. Anyway I went to see André that day. I'd known him for a while, known some of his friends . . . I told him about this guy in my kitchen, and we started talking about the war. It turned out we'd been on the same battlefield together, when he was working as a medic. And I thought, if he starts reminiscing I'll leave. And he said—do you know what he said? I'll never forget it—he said, 'Collective insanity is boring. Individual insanity—that's what interests me.' And I knew that whoever he was, he was different from everyone I'd ever met. He changed me. His ideas were the first thing I was serious about in my life."

"What about the war?" Hélène said. "Weren't you serious about that?"

"The war?" Robert said. "It was a joke. Everyone knew the war would be over in a few months. Sign up now and be home by Christmas. My brother Claude did that, signed up as soon as war was declared, only somehow he managed never to get near the front. My parents were both very patriotic, and I didn't really have any opinions, and when it was my turn I signed up too. But somehow the war went on and on. It was a joke, yes, but a very bad joke, and one that went on far too long. If it wasn't for the fever who knows what would have happened to me? I'd have ended up like that poor fool without his leg."

Hélène yawned. "Go to sleep," Robert said. "Why do you ask me these questions, anyway? I haven't thought about the war for years."

"—interesting—" she said, yawning again. Her eyes closed and she turned over, away from him. She was asleep.

He sat awhile on the bed, watching her slow breathing. Even while he had been talking, his mind had strayed to the recording, and after a while he got up quietly and crossed over to his desk where he'd left it.

He took the record out of the cover and held it carefully between his palms. There was nothing written on the label besides the record's title and the woman's name. Solange. He blew off specks of non-existent dust and cranked up the record player, then put the record gently on the turntable and turned the volume down so as not to wake Hélène. He waited. The turntable spun, he placed the needle carefully on the record. There was no sound, nothing at all. He turned the volume higher, higher still. Nothing happened. He pulled the chair over to the record player and watched amazed as the needle ran through all the grooves on one side, the arm bobbing gently up and down.

At the end he took the record off and looked at it again. The black surface was too shiny, like oil. And the grooves on the record were too close together—maybe that was why his blunt, stubby needle could not call the sounds out of it. He shrugged and turned the record over, putting it back on the turntable.

The other side was silent too. He hummed a little to himself to make sure he hadn't gone deaf. Maybe the record player's broken, he thought, like everything else I've got. He picked up a record at random—Bessie Smith's "Down Hearted Blues"—and set it on the turntable, putting the other one back in the jacket. He had forgotten to turn the volume down and the music when it came shattered the silence. Hélène stirred a little on the bed. He turned the volume down quickly.

He sat for a long while looking at the label through the circle cut on the brown record cover—the words "The Moon's Bright Falling Towers" and a woman's first name. And that was it. No record company, no copyright date, not even a mention of which side was side one. As Bessie Smith sang softly he took out the photograph again, turned it over. The woman—Solange? —wore a bright red dress. He could not remember ever seeing a colored photograph before, and for some reason that frightened him more than anything that had gone before. He set the record down. They painted it, he thought. They painted her dress. He shook his head and turned the music up a little, hoping the strange thoughts would go away.

The music took hold of him as he had hoped it would. For the first time in a long time, prompted by Hélène's questions, he remembered the fever, the strange clean feel of the sheets that he had thought was part of his delirium, the chills, the voices and footsteps, the night sweats when everyone else was asleep. And he remembered the songs coming at odd hours (or were the hours only odd to him, feverish and unused to normal time for so long?), songs about trains and women and being far from home, songs that were never about anything but that vibrated to a single feeling as if to a single chord. When the singer was happy, he was happier than anyone had ever been, and when he was sad, Robert thought he had never heard such sadness. But at the same time, it seemed that the singer understood everything Robert had gone through in the war—the horror and fear of death, the sorrow of being away from home and the different sorrow of never being able to come back. No matter how badly Robert burned in his fever the songs called to him, made him feel rested.

When the fever stopped, the songs did too, and Robert thought at first that they had been part of his delirium. It was several weeks before he could bring himself to ask about them. "The songs?" said one of the nurses. "Oh, you mean the American soldier. He was here for a while, recuperating. A black man." For a minute Robert, still confused by the fever, thought she meant a man made out of ebony and onyx, and then he nodded. "Strange, most of those songs. And they didn't sound—well, they didn't sound very moral." Robert laughed weakly and the nurse went away, offended.

When he left the hospital his wanderings took him to the small but thriving black community growing around Montmartre. No one he knew was interested in blues music, not even André, and even some of the black people he talked to laughed at him for going to their nightclubs. In the past year he had discovered the new recordings, the few—very few—that had made it across the ocean. He went back every month or so, picking up records and trading some of the ones he had. There was something in him that needed the songs, their strange imagery, their uniqueness, their life. Their rhythms made him feel freer.

The record came to an end. He turned off the record player and put the record back into the jacket. Quietly he lifted the photograph and looked at it one last time. Wondering what he had gotten into, longing for company, he went to bed.

Hélène lay still in the light from the lamp. Asleep, without her makeup, she looked defenseless, childlike. For the first time he wondered how old she really was. He wanted to wake her, to ask her to listen to the silent record with him, to look at the colored photograph. Finally he shrugged, turned out the light and went to sleep.

THREE

"Life without dead time."
Graffito, Paris 1968

Antonin waited for Robert the next day outside the Bureau, eyes like mica. "Sorry I'm late," Robert said. "I overslept."

"No problem," Antonin said. He led the way inside.

"Well," Robert said, sitting up on the desk. "What do we do now? Did anything happen?"

"No," Antonin said. He watched Robert intently. "We were waiting for you."

"All right," Robert said. There was no point in trying to talk to Antonin. He stared out the open door.

If the woman were to come back she would be as likely to come here, nexus of probabilities, as anywhere else. The dark-haired woman says good-bye at the station, he thought. Was it poetry if anyone could do it? André would say that that was the point. But was it? A notebook lay open on the desk and he began to draw in it aimlessly, following the curves of the woman's dark hair. A noise made him look up. Three or four people had come in the door.

Antonin stood by the door, his arms crossed. He still regarded Robert with a look approaching fanaticism. Was Robert supposed to be doing something? Antonin did not move. All right, he thought. He jumped down from the desk.

"What's your birthday?" he asked the man closest to him.

"What?" the man said.

"The day of your birth," Robert said. "What is it?"

"Are you an astrologer?" the man asked.

"No," Robert said. "A student of coincidences. An assigner of probabilities. I know the stars and signposts of everyday life, the treasures evoked by the banal. What's your birthday?"

"March eighth," the man said, hesitantly.

"And yours?" he said to another man.

"August first."

"And yours?" to a woman.

"March eighteenth," she said.

"Ten days apart!" Robert said. "What's the probability of that happening, I wonder? Do you two know each other?"

"No," the woman said, amused. The man shrugged.

"And yet you've shared almost your entire lives," Robert said. "He's seen only ten days that you haven't seen. You both have more in common than you and I would ever have. Assuming you were both born the same year, of course. What year were you born, sir?"

"I—" the man said. "Eighteen ninety-three."

"And you?" Robert said to the woman. More people came in the door. "Wait a minute—I have to ask these people. Why don't you come back tonight? We'll talk about life and coincidences and the nature of dreams. Was it just a coincidence that you happened to walk through the door on a day that I would be here? What day were you born, sir?"

The woman laughed and waved good-bye. The man who had just come in the door looked around and said, "November—" Robert had been watching the open doorway absently. Like a page from an old book or a fragment of a dream, she had gone by, the dark-haired woman. He shouted, cutting off the man's reply, and ran out the door. Antonin watched him, nodding slightly as he left.

"Wait!" Robert said, shouting to her. "Wait, I have to talk to you!"

The woman turned back at the shout. Their eyes were at the same level. "It's you!" she said. Her smile made him stand stock-still. "We got through again!"

"Listen," he said, running to catch up with her. "I have to talk to you. Yesterday." He still could not get his breath back. "No, the day before. When I followed you—it was you, wasn't it?—and you told me—"

Lights flashed around them leaving afterimages. He felt the same terrifying sense of disorientation, terrifying to him because never in his life had he been lost for more than a few minutes. The streets stretched out to infinity and then contracted. He waited until they were solid again. "Where was I that night?" he asked. "In the future?"

"Yes," she said. Her voice was musical: he longed

to hear her sing. Ahead of them a woman played a grand piano someone had pulled out into the street. A man and two women sat grouped around the legs of the piano in earnest discussion. Another man had his head in the lap of one of the women: he was asleep.

"But how?" Robert said. He wondered if he was truly going crazy this time. "What's going on?"

They passed the piano, passed two men balancing a ladder in front of an enormous billboard. After some talk, one of the men began to climb the ladder. He was carrying a bucket of paint.

The woman stopped. "Damn," she said. "There's never enough time." She looked down the street, obviously wanting to stay and move on at the same time. "Listen," she said. "We're in the middle of the revolution. I promised my friends I'd help them organize some of the strikers—it's very important and I'm late already—otherwise—" She stopped, moved her hand impatiently. "Believe me, there's nothing I'd like better than to stay and talk to you. I didn't know we'd be able to open the avenues of time again. I could—I'll introduce you to some friends of mine—"

No, he wanted to say. No, stay with me—what's the revolution compared to having a good time? He felt lost, cast adrift in this strange future. She was his anchor.

A young man walked by distributing leaflets. "Minutes," he said to Robert and the woman, handing them each a copy. "What's been decided so far at the Théâtre de l'Odéon, a list of our demands. Come by and give us your opinions."

Robert looked at the piece of paper. He could make no sense of it. He crumpled up the leaflet and threw it on the ground. "Don't do that," the young man said. "The garbage collectors are on strike. We're on our own now."

Robert looked around. The street was festooned with trash like party decorations. He looked at the young man, shrugged and picked up the leaflet.

They began walking again, passing a shop that sold fashionable clothing. Someone had painted across the side of the shop the words "Never work." The woman had gone a little ahead of Robert again and he ran to catch up with her. "Wait," he said. "Where are you taking me?"

"To the Odéon," the woman said. "I'd like you to meet my friends. They don't know that you're from the past—you can tell them or not, whatever you like. I'll try to come back and find you. But I think you'll be interested in the meeting—and they'd probably be interested in your views."

They had come to the Odéon. From inside Robert heard the sound of loud laughter. The theatre had been spray-painted and some of the letters on the front had been removed. They went inside.

Whole rows of seats had been taken out and the curtains torn down. A man up front was talking to a large group of people. Someone shouted to him from the floor. People had stretched out in the aisles or on one of the seats and had gone to sleep or were talking among themselves. The place smelled of wine and stale clothing. And they thought I was crazy, Robert thought. Then he thought, no. They're surrealists. André's won, his ideas have stayed alive. He felt a chill start at the root of his spine and continue up to his hair. He turned to the woman. "What year is it?" he asked her.

"Nineteen sixty-eight," she said. "It's May." She smiled at him for the first time. "You can take your coat off."

A group of people had come up to the woman and started to talk to her animatedly. Robert shrugged his coat off, not listening. "It's ridiculous to talk about the examinations now!" someone on the floor was saying. "We're transforming society, we're not back negotiating with the university. When we're through there will be no university and no exams, no professors and no students."

A few people near the woman who had spoken applauded. The man on the stage continued, unperturbed. "We have to transform society slowly, by stages," he said. "We have to decide what we want from the university, and then where we want to go from there—"

"Reinvent everything!" someone shouted from the floor. "Now!"

More people applauded. "Robert," the woman was saying. Robert looked away from the man on the stage. Near him, on the wall, someone had written, "I am here by the will of the people and I won't leave until I get my raincoat back." "I want you to meet my friends—Patrice, and Gabrielle, and Paul—"

Paul was the man who had tended the fire behind the barricades. In the light he looked different, taller than Robert remembered, his hair almost matching the color of his gold-rimmed glasses. Patrice was shorter than Paul, his round face and glasses—very nearly the same as Paul's—giving him the look of an intent, slightly drunken owl. Gabrielle had long, very beautiful reddish-brown hair. Robert nodded slightly to Paul. "We've met," he said.

"Did you ever find the woman you were looking for?" Paul asked. "The one you were asking about that night?"

Robert laughed shortly. "I did," he said. "But I don't think she'll stay found."

The dark-haired woman laughed. "I have to go help some friends of mine," she said to Paul. "And we'll need help with the food distribution tonight, if you can get away—"

"I'll see," Paul said. "It'll depend on what happens here."

"All right," the woman said. "I've really got to go. You two should get to know each other. Robert's interested in surrealism." She smiled at Robert again, a private smile, and turned to go.

"Good-bye, Solange," he called after her. She did not acknowledge the name; she didn't deny it either. He wanted to run after her, to help her with the strikers, the food distribution, anything she wanted just to be near her. But she had made it clear she was leaving him with her friends. They were already sitting down on the sticky floor. He sighed and sat near them.

"You're interested in surrealism?" Paul said. He had been watching Robert intently. Was he too in love with Solange? "In what aspect?"

"In the aspect of play, I suppose," Robert said. What if he told these people where he was from? They'd think he was crazy. The situation was complicated enough. He wondered where Solange had gone, his mind not really on his answer to Paul.

"Yes, of course," Paul said seriously. "But what of surrealism's revolutionary content? Of the surrealists' desire to change life?"

"The desire to play *is* revolutionary," Gabrielle said.

"I know that," Paul said. "I meant—"

"You know that intellectually," Gabrielle said. "When was the last time you—"

"What do you mean by revolutionary content?" Patrice said suddenly. "Surrealism—the surrealists—couldn't sustain their revolutionary beliefs in the end—"

51

"What do you mean?" Robert said. He felt as if he had been plunged into ice water, cut off, isolated, out of his time. What had happened to his friends in the intervening years? "André—André Breton—would never—" He stopped. Suppose even André had compromised in the end? He tried to imagine his friend wearing a modest business suit and failed.

"No, Breton never compromised," Patrice said. "Breton and a few of the others. But for the most part I think we have to consider surrealism a failed movement. What about Aragon, what about Eluard—"

"What about Dali?" Paul said. Robert looked at him, glad of the interruption. He hadn't wanted to know what had happened to his close friends. And what if they started talking about him? He was about to ask who Dali was when Patrice spoke again.

"But that's not really the point," he said. "Breton wanted to change the world. And he failed—he didn't. He failed to set the world on fire. In fact he—"

"But that wasn't his fault!" Robert said. He wondered briefly why he was defending André so passionately. "How can you blame that on him? The world didn't want to be changed. And look at you—look at all of you. More than forty years after the beginning of surrealism, you're defending the principles André fought for, lived his life for. You weren't even born then."

"He has a point, Patrice," Gabrielle said, grinning sardonically.

"Does he?" Paul said. "It remains to be seen how successful we are here."

"That's not really important," Gabrielle said. "We're proving that surrealism is never really dead. It may go underground for years and years—look at what happened to Breton during the war, for example—but it will always resurface."

What war? Robert thought. Suddenly he didn't want to hear any more. "Listen," he said. "Is this all you do? Sit around and talk about dead art movements? I mean, is this the revolution?"

"We have to go talk to the workers at the factories!" someone on the stage was saying, as if in response to Robert's question. "Staying here accomplishes nothing. We have to support the general strike!"

"We tried that," someone on the floor said tiredly. "They wouldn't let us in."

"Well, naturally they're suspicious of students—"

"Students, hell. They just wanted higher wages, they didn't want to talk to us at all—"

"No, not really," Gabrielle said to Robert. "Sometimes we sleep, too." She smiled her sardonic grin at him and gestured at the bodies sprawled out in the theatre. "Sitting and talking is hard work."

"Some people contribute more when they're asleep," Paul said.

"That's probably true," Gabrielle said. "Did you see the graffiti that said, 'Form dream committees'?"

Paul sighed. "I get so sick of all this goddamn graffiti," he said. "Everyone's an artist all of a sudden."

"Everyone *is*," Gabrielle said simply. Robert heard the echo of André in her voice, and suddenly wished he could take her back with him. André would want to meet her.

"Everyone's a bad artist, then," Paul said.

"Listen," Patrice said. "They're about to go march to the Renault factory."

People in the front rows were standing, stretching. "Let's go," Patrice said.

"Do you think it'll do any good?" Paul said. "You heard what they said—"

"More good than it'll do staying here," Patrice said, standing up. "Come on."

Paul stood up too. "I don't know," Gabrielle said. She looked from Paul and Patrice to Robert and back again. "All right. Are you coming?"

"I suppose so," Robert said. He looked at the door nervously, hoping to see Solange. He was getting tired of waiting. "Let's go somewhere. I have nothing else to do."

"That's right," Patrice said, laughing shortly. "Why I joined the revolution. 'Well, I had nothing better to do on my summer vacation . . .' "

"I didn't mean—" Robert said. Gabrielle was saying, "Hey, guys, that's not fair—"

"You're right," Patrice said. "It's not. I'm sorry. I don't even know you."

"That's all right," Robert said.

They were walking out of the theatre now, stepping over clothes and litter. Robert blinked a little in the sunlight. He wondered where the Renault factory was. Someone at the front picked a direction and they began to walk. Robert found himself next to Gabrielle.

"How do you know Solange?" he asked her as casually as possible.

Gabrielle looked at him sharply. "Oh hell," she said. "Of all the questions you could have asked, you had to pick that one. . . . Paul and I used to be lovers. That is, until he met her."

"Oh," Robert said. "I'm sorry." But less for you than for me, he thought. Jealousy flamed within him. So that was why Paul had acted so strangely, the night he had first blundered into the future and asked for her. But what did Solange feel for Paul? And why had she come for him in the first place? He was a little shocked, too, that Gabrielle would talk about her affairs so openly. A few of the surrealists did, but none of the women, at least none that he knew of. They passed a closed police station. Someone had written on the wall, "It is forbidden to forbid."

A few people at the front of the line began to sing and he tried to follow the melody. "What do you do?" Gabrielle asked him.

"Me?" Robert said, drawn out of his thoughts. He stopped a moment to light a cigarette. "Nothing."

"Are you a student?" she said.

"No," he said. He laughed. "I was a student a long time ago. It didn't work out."

"So you really don't—" Gabrielle said. Robert shook his head. "I guess you really are a surrealist then."

Robert laughed again, joyfully. He felt elated suddenly, walking in the sharp spring air of Paris, reprieved for the moment from winter. Someone standing in the street handed him and Gabrielle green apples from a box. Reprieved from poverty. Someone else gave him a salute he didn't recognize. The wind lifted his hair. He was free.

"That's important," Gabrielle said thoughtfully. "Not having a job. If you could—if we could just set up this society intelligently, people wouldn't have to work more than two, three hours a day. You'd be free to do whatever you wanted. Those two—Paul and Patrice—they're great talkers, but I don't think they understand what we're trying to do here. Paul— Maybe I'm just cynical, but I don't think Paul cares about anything but his own future. And before the strike, all Patrice ever did was sit in cafés and write political manifestos. Of course Patrice is a good person to have on your side. Though a bit fanatic, I sometimes think. And Paul's heart is probably in the right place," she added quickly, trying to be fair.

"I don't—I don't really think of myself as a revolutionary," he said, trying to be truthful. "I just want to have a good time."

"Well," Gabrielle said simply, brushing her long hair out of her eyes, "that's why we're doing this."

She was silent for a long time. He walked beside her thoughtfully, listening to the songs borne back by the wind. What would the factory workers do if Gabrielle told them all to go home and play? Laugh at her, probably, or ask her how they could negotiate for higher wages. Was it true that working only two or three hours a day was all that was needed? Perhaps technology had changed since his time. He felt, and was ashamed of himself for feeling, a small stab of envy. If no one else worked he would lose his special status, insulted by concierges, shunned by waiters, free to go anywhere and do anything, hemmed only by his imagination. Would the others, the great mass of workers, understand their sudden freedom? Probably not. But it was a wonderful dream.

They passed overturned cars, torn pavement, trees just beginning to bud pulled up from the sidewalks. Gabrielle shook her head. "It's strange," she said. "Seeing the streets like this. It's like a dream—it's real, but it's unreal too. Where did all these barricades come from? The city's changed overnight. We dreamed it, and it changed."

"I know what you mean," Robert said. Unknowingly, she had captured everything he had been thinking. He wondered how much he could tell her. "It's completely different. There are parts of Paris I don't even recognize."

"You know what everybody says?" Gabrielle said. "Whether we win or lose, everybody says that nothing will ever be the same. That's how I feel. One minute we're all going calmly to work or to school, keeping the wheels turning, and the next minute we're all on strike. Millions of people, all over the country, on strike. Just knowing that it can be done has changed everything. We've punched a hole in reality."

"You're right," Robert said. Was that how he had come here? He tried to follow the thought but it eluded him. "It seems as though anything could happen now."

The line of marchers had stopped for some reason. The sun came out from behind the clouds, turning the streets silver. "I was talking to a friend of mine," Gabrielle said. "She'd gotten married, had children—we'd sort of lost touch. I ran into her just a few days ago and she told me she and her husband had bought a car. Then she stopped a bit, and she said, 'You know, it's ridiculous to work all your life for things like that—a car, a house.' But she's always believed in that, ever since I've known her. We've changed the way she thinks, changed her reality. You're right—anything can happen now."

"Look!" Robert said, pointing down the street. A group of people had moved a dining table out into the street and were sitting around it eating and talking. Were they protesting something, perhaps an eviction, or were they celebrating the absurdity of the moment? He laughed. Everyone is a surrealist, he thought. We just do what everyone would do if they could. As they watched, a reporter came up to the group, took out a pad of paper and a pen and began to ask them questions. With great solemnity someone at the table began to butter the reporter's tie. The reporter stepped back.

The marchers were moving again. As they passed the group around the table, Robert saluted them and someone saluted back with a chicken leg. "It's amazing," Gabrielle said. "How quickly they've understood the spirit of things. A student rebellion, a few pamphlets . . . But I guess everyone already understood what we were trying to do. If only we had known it would be so easy. Everyone's on strike now. The chorus girls at the Folies-Bergère. The bank tellers—do you know how hard it is to get any money right now?" She laughed. "Even the fortune-tellers."

"But that's—that's wonderful!" Robert said. "I met a fortune-teller once who said she would go on strike. On strike for belief, for dreams. I wonder if she's here now. Maybe she foretold all this."

"I'm glad I'm not missing this," Gabrielle said. "I'm glad I'm alive now."

"I'm glad—" Robert said, then stopped. How could the fortune-teller be here? How could *he* be here? The feeling of elation had gone as quickly as it had come. A cold wind blew over him. Perhaps he would not be alive in this time. Nineteen sixty-eight was a long way away from his life, his friends. The marchers had stopped. They had come to the factory doors.

Crowds of people stood out in front of the factory. A few chanted something he couldn't hear. In that large a group, he shouldn't have been able to spot her but he did. She always seemed to be surrounded by a clear space, a golden light. She had put a red rose in her hair. He pushed his way through the crowd, ignoring Gabrielle, until he reached her. "Hello again, Solange," he said.

She turned to him. "Hello, Robert!" she said. He could warm himself by the fire of her smile, by the redness of her rose. "It's good to see you here. Just a minute." She began talking to a small, intense-looking man by her side. "What do you think? Someone will have to go in and talk to them. Should we vote on it?

It'll have to be someone who understands what's going on in there."

Robert sighed. For the first time he felt himself resenting her. Was it always going to be this way? Would he always be pushed to the background, ignored, forced to wait for her? All he wanted was to talk to her, to touch her. If she summoned him again could he refuse?

He turned his attention to the crowd in front of the factory doors. He resented them, too, for coming between him and Solange. Suddenly he didn't care if the revolution were lost or won, only that it be over. Gabrielle stood near the front, talking to Paul and shaking her head fiercely. Patrice left both of them and went up to the doors, looking full of purpose. Four young men carrying wooden planks walked to the front of the crowd and began to set up a stage.

Robert frowned, trying to see them clearly. Was it a dance, a magic trick, a ritual? In the brightness of the May sun they seemed to shimmer slightly, as though falling through clear water. He looked once at Solange to make sure she hadn't disappeared, then tilted his head to see the players better.

They had metal rings they passed to one another, cones of light, colored scarves, golden stars. At times they seemed part of a vast intricate play full of intrigue and false starts. At other times they could have been onlookers who had somehow wandered up on stage: fumbling with scarves and bits of clothing or staring out over the crowd, still as statues. Then they would suddenly toss the golden stars or juggle and begin again. Everything was done in silence, but Robert could hear the clank of the rings even over the noise of the crowd. Once someone came up from among the demonstrators and took a bright scarf, and one of the players went down into the crowd.

Robert looked at Solange again, seeking explanations. The small, intense man had apparently been chosen to talk to the workers in the factory. He walked up to the factory door and raised his hand to knock. A sudden movement from one of the players distracted Robert and he looked away. A metal ring had been thrown into the air, higher, higher, diminishing quickly against the sky but still sparkling as sharply as diamonds. The small man knocked. The ring disappeared.

Someone screamed or cried out. A fifth man had appeared among the players, a man wearing a mask of horns and fur and metal, a fantastic mingling of animal and machine. The players jumped from the stage. Robert strained to see clearer. Was that really a mask? Where was it joined to his body? He shuddered, seeing a creature come fresh from his nightmares, from the dreams he could never remember in sunlight. The man raised his hand and the earth rocked. More people screamed.

Solange, Robert thought at once. He searched the crowd, panicked, looking for her. People were scattering in every direction, trying to get away, trying to get toward the factory. There she was, running for the factory doors. The earth shook again and she fell to the ground. He ran to help her, not thinking. He heard shots, saw trails of smoke. As he reached her the smoke blew white, blinding him. It cleared—

—He was standing in front of the Bureau of Surrealistic Research, coughing. Antonin came outside and watched as he tried to get his breath back. "And when were you born?" Antonin asked. "What year?"

Robert coughed one last time, wiping his eyes on his sleeve. He realized he had left his coat back at the theatre. Back in the future. He began to shiver in the winter wind. "Where—" he began. Antonin was obviously expecting something. The sun was slanting down toward night. He had missed another whole day of work. "What time is it?"

"It's 1924," Antonin said.

Robert looked at him suspiciously. What did he know? "Never mind that," he said. "Is it five yet? Are we about to close up?"

"Past five," Antonin said. "I was waiting for you."

"Why?" Robert said, still trying to clear his head. He knew Antonin would never ask him where he'd been. Was it part of his madman's game or did he really know something?

"That's why we're here," Antonin said. "Research. Recording of surrealistic events. Something happens to you and you write it down."

"You're saying—" Robert said. Antonin did not answer. "What?"

"Write down your experiences," Antonin said. In the dimming light, Robert could not see his expression.

"What experiences?" Robert said. "I saw someone I recognized and left. That's all."

"Write it down," Antonin said. "Where you went, what you did, who you saw. That's why we're here. The notebook is on the desk."

"All right," Robert said. There was no way around it. He would have to either make something up or tell the truth. "I'll tell you what," he said. "Leave me the keys and I'll stay here and write."

Antonin handed him the keys. Robert took a deep breath and went inside. The place was empty. He sat behind the desk for a while, looking at the notebook in front of him. If he wrote that he had simply gone for a walk, André would be angry at him. If he told the truth, though, it wouldn't matter. André would assume he had made everything up to get out of working at the Bureau. Maybe André would even want to publish it in the magazine. Robert laughed and pulled the notebook toward him.

He looked awhile at the lines he had sketched just that morning, the wavy hair like diagrams of electrical fields. Where was she now? What was she doing? Would he see her again? Somehow he knew that he would. He emptied his mind of speculation and began to write, slowly at first and then as fast as he could as the words came to him. He wrote it all down—his meeting with the dark-haired woman, his visit to the theatre, the factory, the four players and the man in the fantastic mask. It was dark outside the storefront when he finally finished and closed the notebook. He stood up, stretched and turned off the lights. The mannequin was a dark spot against the ceiling. He locked the door and struck a match, lighting a cigarette, then set out for home. It was still early evening but he wanted to sleep. He would decide what to do in the morning.

FOUR

"Leave everything. . . .
Leave your wife leave your mistress.
Leave your hopes and your fears.
Sow your children in the corner of a wood.
Leave the substance for the shadow. . . .
Set out on the road."
André Breton

The woman opened her mouth to scream, sound-lessly. The man in black flattened himself against the window, beckoning to her. The woman screamed again, her neck white as the curve of the moon. "Come on," André whispered in the darkness. "Let's go."

"Wait a minute," Robert said, whispering back. The images continued to flicker against the movie screen. "What happens next?"

"Let's go," André said again. "The plot isn't important. The images, the juxtapositions—that's what we want to see."

They left the theatre, walked two blocks and went into another building. A man on the screen stood poised against the snow, ready to hurl a spear. Snowflakes caught in his hood, his fur breeches. "Let's go," André said. They hadn't even sat down.

"Now wait—" Robert said. The spear shot against the sky, arching like the woman's neck had arched a moment ago. "What is this? Where are we—Antarctica?"

"You can't ask those questions," André said impatiently, walking out of the theatre. "I should have brought Louis instead. Where's the next theatre, over this way?"

"No," Robert said. "Two blocks to the right." He began to walk eagerly, hurrying toward the next image, suddenly understanding, after an afternoon spent in darkened theatres, André's game. The discontinuous images had flashed without ceasing against his eyes, unreeling themselves from the great fabric woven and dyed in the factories of dreams in America. Paris in daylight now seemed unreal, louder, more colorful, yet somehow a shadow of what happened on the movie screens. "Come on," he said.

Sherlock Holmes stood at the front of the screen, puffing on his pipe and talking. Suddenly he turned and pointed to a note lying on a coffee table. A man looked on in horror. The film cut to a black subtitle. "We don't want to know what they're saying," André said. "Movies should be silent, like dreams. Let's go."

Someone near André said, "Quiet, please!"

"Quiet?" André said, oilily polite. Only Robert knew how close to anger he was. "What do you want to hear, the noise of the projector? Come on, let's go."

"Where's the next theatre?" André asked after they had stepped out into the streets again. "Is it very far from here?"

"About a mile," Robert said, hands jingling loose

change in his pockets. "Look, André, I don't really have much money left. And what I do have has got to last me until the end of the month which is—" He paused, considering. He had lost all track of time since he had come back from the future.

"Only next week," André said. "One more movie and then we'll stop."

"No, I can't," Robert said, wanting to go with him, hating to stop the urgent momentum of the black-and-white pictures. "Really."

"All right," André said. "What about a drink, then? Do you have enough money for that?"

"Of course," Robert said, grinning at him. "There's a good café just about a block from here. Let's go."

The café was dark and almost empty in the late afternoon. "I'm getting a little worried about Antonin," André said without preliminary, sitting back and sipping his drink.

"Antonin?" Robert said. "Do you think he's dangerous? Most of his craziness is just an act, I think."

"No, it's not that," André said. "I don't mind that some people would call him crazy. That's one of the reasons I admitted him to the group, in fact."

"Then what?" Robert said. "He's working very hard at making the Bureau what you wanted it to be."

"I know," André said. "He's just—well, he's becoming too commercial."

"What do you mean?" Robert said, confused. "The Bureau?"

"No," André said. He shook his head, took another sip of his drink. "Antonin. He's acting in plays, wants to get into movies. He even has plans to start a theatre himself some day."

"But what's wrong with that?" Robert said. "Maybe he should get into movies. Someday I'd like to walk into a theatre and see his face up there along with the others—Sherlock Holmes, and the guy throwing the spear . . ."

"He doesn't take surrealism seriously," André said. "All he sees are commercial possibilities. We aren't an art movement but a movement to change the world. We aren't surrealists to make money."

"No, of course not," Robert said. He lit a cigarette and drew on it. "But Antonin? He's spent every day this week at the Bureau. Certainly not for money."

André shook his head. "I don't like the idea of his acting," he said. "I don't like the theatre. I don't want surrealism to become commercial, a commodity like everything else. What I don't like, what is loathsome, is the fact that we're becoming accepted. The bourgeoisie accepts us."

Robert shrugged. "I don't know," he said. "No one's accepted me yet. If we're acceptable my concierge still doesn't know about it."

"How is your writing going, anyway?" André said. "I enjoyed what you wrote for the Bureau. It had a strong dreamlike quality."

Robert coughed and took a long puff on his cigarette to cover his confusion. "I don't know," he said. "I mean—I haven't written anything since that." He took a final puff on the cigarette and ground it out. "But you know—" he said, narrowing his eyes in the darkness of the café, wondering how much he could trust his old friend—"a lot of that—well—I didn't make it up. A lot of it really happened."

"Well, of course," André said. "Surely you didn't think I wanted a piece of fiction? A made-up story with a straight-forward narrative?"

"What I mean is—" Robert said. "A lot of the things that seem as though they were made up—I mean the things that seem the most dreamlike—they were real. They really happened." His heart was pounding. There. He had said it.

"I don't know why people think we're only interested in dreams, in the unconscious," André said. "What we're really interested in is the state where dreams and reality, the conscious and the unconscious *meet*. That's where you find the truth. Like in mythology—primitive mythologies, not our horrible modern versions, God knows."

Robert watched him closely. Would he stop lecturing for a while and talk to him, friend to friend? The strangest event of his life had happened, the pivotal event about which he could no more stop thinking than he could stop breathing, and André had somehow managed to turn it into a talk about surrealist theory. Robert wanted to stop him, to ask for advice, for help. He looked at his old friend across the table again, carefully. No. He wouldn't beg.

"What do you mean?" Robert asked as casually as he could. He felt as though André, his longtime mentor, were taking some crucially important test.

"I mean that the writing was very good," André said. "Your experience—the experience that inspired it—was a genuine surrealist experience. An encounter between dream and reality. That's what we're trying to do. That's why we opened the Bureau. I hope you'll let me know if you write anything more."

"I don't think—I don't really think that that's my style of writing," Robert said, still casual. André had failed the test. His friend had gone away from him, retreated into a thicket of theories and ideas. The break would come soon. He spoke slowly, choosing his words with care. "What I want to write about—I want to write about Paris. Paris as a character. And everyone else, too—the pickpockets, the prostitutes, the musicians, the gypsies—all the people who come out at night. A novel about Paris at night," he said animatedly.

"A novel?" André laughed. "The novel's dead—don't waste your time. The novel takes a small—oh, infinitely small—cut-and-dried section of so-called reality and calls it art. Your life is art. Don't waste it trying to write a novel." He gripped his heavy cane and stood up, dismissing Robert's idea. "Are you going to be at the café tonight?"

"The café?" Robert said. "No, I don't think so. I'll see you." He stood up and they left the café without saying good-bye.

Snow was beginning to fall as he headed toward his apartment. He huddled down into the jacket André had given him to replace the one he'd lost. As usual André had been generous, and as usual his generosity had gone awry—the damn sleeves were too short. For a moment Robert wondered bitterly if surrealism would have occupied such an important part of André's life had he been a little taller.

Robert turned down a small side street. Winter was settling down over Paris, which meant he'd have to fix his small heater, which meant a large part of next month's check was already spent. He sighed. What was he doing running his life like this? Maybe it was time to settle down, get some kind of job. He was certainly old enough. Like a man who can't keep from probing a rotten tooth, he thought for the thousandth time of a job and for the thousandth time rejected the idea. I can't be anywhere on time, he thought. I can't take orders, not even from those communists André was mixed up with a few months back. I can't learn something I don't enjoy, I can't stick with things, I can't be responsible. The list clicked off in his mind. He turned

the collar of the jacket up and tried again to pull the
sleeves down, then laughed as a new thought came to
him. In the future, he thought, they are fighting for the
kind of life I live now.

He walked up the steps of his apartment, wondering if the bread he had bought a week ago was still
good. All right, he thought. All right, tomorrow I'll try
the publishers, see if someone needs a proofreader . . .
Louis might know someone. "M. St. Onge?" someone
said, interrupting his thoughts. He looked up. It was
the concierge.

"Yes?" he said.

"Telegram," she said. "For you."

"Thank you," he said, surprised. He stood on the
steps of the apartment building and opened the envelope, trying to conceal the message from the concierge.
"PLEASE COME HOME MOTHER," it said. There
was nothing else.

He turned the envelope over and back again, searching for clues. "From Nice," the concierge said, trying to
be helpful.

"It is," he said neutrally.

"Well," the concierge said. "I guess I'd better be
getting back to my work." Her manner was a little more
respectful. People who got telegrams, especially telegrams from Nice, were a step up from the class she had
thought Robert belonged to.

"I guess you'd better," he said. He still did not
move. Why would his mother want to speak to him
now?

Georges shifted the roadster into fourth and pulled
the steering wheel to the right, putting his whole body
into the turn. The car narrowly missed a horse grazing
by the side of the road. "Are you sure your parents

won't mind your bringing a friend?" he asked, shouting over the noise of the wind and the motor.

"What?" Robert said, shouting back.

"Are you sure your parents won't mind?" Georges said. They took another turn. Robert gripped the side of the windshield to steady himself. "Are you frightened?" Georges said, taking his eyes away from the road to look at him.

"No," Robert said. "It's too early in the morning." The wind burned his ears. "Let's keep going—I want to get there as soon as we can."

They had come up behind a farmer driving his cart to market. Georges downshifted and stayed behind the cart for a moment, then suddenly honked his horn—the horn he had stolen from a taxi cab and mounted outside the car—and swerved around the cart in one movement. The driver of the cart opened his mouth to say something, Georges honked at him again, and then they were gone.

Discontinuous images, Robert thought. Things moving too fast to stay in the mind. André would have enjoyed this trip. He wished he was awake enough to enjoy it—they had left early that morning, at nine o'clock. He was too tired even to feel the cold, though at least the snow had stopped. "No, I don't think they'd mind," Robert said. "I've brought friends home before." He wondered again why his mother had sent the telegram and what she wanted to say to him. If it was private family business she probably wouldn't want Georges there. But she wouldn't be able to argue with him in front of a friend. "I'm glad I ran into you last night," Robert said. "If it wasn't for you I'd have had to take the train." Georges was on the fringes of the movement, friends with several of the surrealists.

"I'm glad you did too," Georges said. "It isn't

every day I get to take a vacation like this." He looked at Robert and grinned, then pulled his cap down and they sped around another curve.

At dusk they pulled over to the side of the road and looked for a place to sleep. "That field looks dry enough, I guess," Georges said. He looked at Robert critically. "Is that jacket going to be warm enough for you?"

Robert pulled down the sleeves in what was becoming a habitual gesture. "I think so," he said. He lit a cigarette and opened the door on his side of the car. "There's really no choice, is there?"

"Look!" Georges said suddenly. "Over there."

"What?"

"Over there," Georges said, motioning with his chin. "The church."

"What about—" Robert said. "Oh. Do you think we should sleep there?"

"Sure," Georges said. "Why not?"

Robert pulled on the cigarette for the last time and threw it out of the car. "Some surrealist," Georges said. "Wait until I tell André. You'll be thrown out of the movement."

"Sure, let's go," Robert said. "But do me a favor, all right? Let's keep André out of this. I'm driving all the way across France to escape him—I don't need you to lecture me on surrealist morality." His tone was harsher than he'd meant it to be.

"I'm sorry—" Georges said.

"No, don't be sorry," Robert said impatiently. He stepped out of the car, stretching his legs. "I had an argument with him before we left, that's all. Let's go."

"An argument?" Georges said. "About what? I thought you two were friends."

"We are," Robert said. "Or we were. Sometimes I

get the feeling that I've outgrown him. That everything's changed but him."

"Oh," Georges said. "Well, he can be a little—" he paused—"immobile."

Robert laughed. Georges took a small valise from the trunk and they started across the fields toward the church. "Surrealist morality," Georges said. "That's good. 'It is the highest morality to sleep in a church whenever possible,' " he said, imitating André's pedantic way of speaking. " 'Any surrealist who fails to do so must atone for his sin by—' "

"Reciting all of André's poems."

"Backwards."

They walked on in silence for a while. "I'll tell you one of the things I'm tired of," Robert said finally. "Everything André does he does for political reasons. To shock someone. I don't want to sleep in a church if there has to be a reason behind it. I just want to have a good time."

"You are having a good time," Georges said. "You're not sleeping out in the fields." In the dark Robert nodded thoughtfully. They reached the church and Georges put his hand on the doorknob. "Your problem," he said, "is that you're too close to André." He turned the knob and pulled on the door. It opened. Georges bowed to Robert and followed him in. "You should try to be more like me. I'm friendly with some of the same people, but I don't take the ideas seriously." He closed the door behind them.

"It's different with me," Robert said. "André's my oldest and closest friend. If I left him now it would have to be a clean break." He took out a cigarette, shrugged and lit it.

"Look at that," Georges said, whispering. By the rays of the setting sun they could see a crudely drawn mural of Christ on the cross. "What if we added a bit to it—a couple over here making love in the corner—"

"What?" Robert said, mock-horrified. "Realism in art?"

Georges laughed. "You—you didn't bring any luggage, did you?" he said.

"No," Robert said. He opened his jacket, closed it again. "This is it."

"I have—I have an extra jacket, if you'd like," Georges said. "I brought a blanket for myself."

"Sure, if it's all right with you," Robert said. "Thanks." He suddenly warmed toward Georges, who had not asked him why he was so poor and his parents were so rich. It's no wonder everyone likes Georges, he thought, taking the jacket and spreading it on the floor. Georges gets along with everyone. Well, so do I. He pulled the jacket around him, trying to get comfortable. Everyone except my friends. And my family. And my concierge. "Good night," he said. He stubbed his cigarette out against the floor. In the empty, darkening church he felt somehow at home, surrounded by friends.

"Good night," Georges said.

They arrived in Nice at noon the next day. Robert, who had slept for most of the last leg of the journey, woke up to give directions. "A left here," he said. "Right down this street. It's on this street somewhere, but I don't remember what it looks like. Just a minute. There's a wrought iron gate around the front."

"When was the last time you were there?" Georges asked, downshifting and turning around in the middle of the street. An old woman bundled up in furs walked past and Georges honked the horn at her. She didn't turn around.

"Last year," Robert said.

"Last *year*?" Georges said. "And you can't remember what it looks like?"

"Or maybe the year before," Robert said. "I can't remember. I try not to think about them when I'm away from home."

"Oh," Georges said. "What are your parents like, anyway?"

"There it is," Robert said. "That house over there. See it? The one back away from the street."

"All right," Georges said. He pulled over and stopped the car. "What wrought iron fence?"

"Well, there's iron somewhere," Robert said. He looked haggard, unshaven. "Maybe a bannister or something." Georges gave him a strange look and got out of the car.

There was a small iron handrail beside the stairs to the front door. As they crossed the lawn, Robert pointed to a marble statue of a young girl and a deer. "When I was younger," he said, surprised at the vividness of the memory, "I thought that statue could talk."

"Which one," Georges said, "the girl or the deer?"

"I don't remember," Robert said, distracted, realizing that he had not told Georges the whole truth. When he was younger, he had thought that everything could talk, that everything was alive and had a voice. That if he was very good he might be able to hear them, that once, long ago, he had heard them. He started to climb the stairs to the front door, the memories coming back. He remembered telling his older brother Claude what the tree in the garden had said to him, and the beating he had gotten from Claude for not believing in the Church. "You don't understand!" Robert had said, crying, thinking that Claude had meant a building when he had said the Church. "The Church

talks too! You just have to be good, to be very good—"
Claude had only hit him harder.

Robert shook his head to set free the memories.
Was that when he had begun to doubt everything he'd
been told, to believe no one's truth but his own? It's no
wonder I became a surrealist, he thought. He waited
for a while at the top of the stairs and then rang the
bell.

A woman dressed in black opened the door and
looked out, then opened the door wider. "Mother,"
Robert said. "This is my friend—"

"Hello," Madame St. Onge said. She took Robert's
hand and glanced quickly, neutrally, at Georges. "What
have you been up to? You look as though you've been
sleeping in the gutter."

"In churches," Robert said. "This is Georges, my
friend."

"Hello, Georges," Madame St. Onge said. "I thought
this would be just a family gathering."

"I never would have made it here if it hadn't been
for him," Robert said. "I didn't have money for the
train."

"I would have wired you money," Madame St.
Onge said. "Please." She released his hand. "Have one
of the servants draw you a bath. And I suppose you'll
need someone to carry your luggage. Alain!"

"I don't have any luggage," Robert said. "And
Georges just has his bag."

"That's all right," Georges said. "I should probably
go back to Paris anyway."

"Oh, no," Madame St. Onge said. "I suppose it's
all right. Georges can have the spare bedroom. No—
that'll be taken. Well then, he can stay with you, in
your room. I wish you had phoned me when you got
my telegram, that's all. You see, last week your father

had a rather bad stroke. And then yesterday—well, yesterday morning he passed away. The funeral will be tomorrow." And she turned and walked into the dim interior of the house.

"I'm going home," Georges said. "Are you all right?"

"No," Robert said. "I mean, I'm all right, but you can't go home. I'd appreciate it if you didn't go home. You don't have to go to the funeral. Just—keep me company. Please."

Georges took a long breath. "Sure," he said. He picked up the valise. "Let's go. Where's your room?"

They went inside the house together. "Are you sure you're all right?" Georges asked again. "I mean—your father . . ."

"I don't know," Robert said. "I mean—I barely remember him. Like this house." He gestured in front of him as they climbed the stairs. But the house was starting to seem more familiar to him now—the Oriental carpets, the potted plants, the closed curtains and the lights that were always too dim. "In a moment I'll think of something good to say about my father. He left me alone. There, how's that?"

Robert opened the first door on the left. "This is my room." He pressed the light switch. The room seemed larger than his entire apartment. The heavy furniture—the bed, the desk, the chairs—had not changed since his last visit. "The ones across the hall are for my brother and sister—Claude and Noelle. You'll meet them, I guess."

They walked into the room and sat on the carefully made bed. Georges set the valise by his feet. "No, it's her," Robert said. "The way she likes to cut the ground out in front of me. She always did that, always. You tell her you slept in a church and she tells you your father died. You can never win with her."

Georges nodded. He looked polite but confused. "How long—" he said. A man knocked on the open door and stepped inside. "Your mother wants to know if you've had a bath, sir," the man said. "And then she'd like to see you in the library." His eyes flickered briefly over Georges. "Alone." He bowed slightly and left.

"Well," Robert said. "This is it."

"Good luck," Georges said. "Don't let her get to you."

"I'll try," said Robert.

Madame St. Onge sat behind the heavy oak desk that had been his father's. How typical, Robert thought, stepping into the room. With no warning at all, grief welled up within him. He would never see his father sitting behind that desk again.

"Good afternoon, Robert," his mother said. "Sit down, please."

He remained standing. She ignored him and went on. "I know your father's—death must come as a terrible shock to you," she said. She does have feelings then, Robert thought, grateful for the slight pause before the word "death." "But there's a great deal of business to take care of before the funeral, before everyone starts to arrive. So. Are you sure you don't want to sit down?"

Robert shook his head. He was beginning to feel uncomfortable standing. "All right then," his mother said. "As you know, your father and I have provided you with an allowance since you were eighteen." Robert nodded. What is she getting at? he thought. Oh. The will. "What you may not know is that I was very much opposed to this allowance from the beginning." He nodded again, not surprised. "I believe in hard work, in earning what you get. So. It is now the end of November. You will get your allowance for the month of December. But that is all. It is time to go out into the real world, Robert, time to get a job."

Robert said nothing. "I'd like to hear what your plans are," his mother said. "Of course, I'd be happy to help you out in terms of—a career." She was faltering, the last sentence almost a question. "You always were the difficult one in the family," she said, back on familiar ground.

"I don't know," Robert said finally. "I hear gambling's pretty good around here. Maybe I'll look into that."

She sighed. "Don't be foolish," she said. "Some day you'll learn you have to grow up."

"Well, I don't know then," he said. "I can't have a career." To his horror he sounded as though he were begging. "I'm a poet, a—a writer. That's my career."

"Yes, of course," his mother said. "Look at that jacket you're wearing. That's where being a poet gets you."

"It isn't even mine," he said hotly. This is absurd, he thought. How did I get trapped into defending André's jacket?

"Of course not," she said. "You don't even have the money for a jacket."

"And you don't even know anyone who would give you a jacket," he said. "Who do you think is poorer, you or me?"

"I didn't mean to start an argument—"

"No, because you'd lose if you did—"

"I am simply telling you my intentions," she said, standing up and walking around the desk. "What you do now is your business. Good day." She left the room.

"Good day," he said, calling after her. He was shaking.

After she had gone Robert went around the desk

and sat in the chair that had been his father's. He opened the top drawer and began to look through the papers idly. Shipping receipts. Construction invoices. A letter from a winery. It occurred to him that he didn't even know where his family's money came from, the money he had spent so blithely on drinks and strange headdresses and blues recordings. And now all that would come to an end. What would he do?

Claude came into the room without knocking. "I've been thinking about your future, young man," Robert said, still sitting behind the desk. "I've decided it would be best for you—best for the entire family—if you became—say, a shepherd. I can give you money for a warm coat and a pair of fleecing shears, but that's all. It's time for you to grow up, you know."

"She's talked to you already, has she?" Claude said.

"Yes, she has," Robert said. He noticed he was still holding one of the pieces of paper and he put it back in the drawer. "I suppose you're going to take over the family business now?"

"That's right," Claude said, nodding pleasantly. "What do you think? I can use a partner, someone willing to learn. You might even be able to stay in Paris."

Robert put his feet up on the desk. "I don't even know what the business is," he said. He thought of Rimbaud, trader in darkest Africa. The idea still did not appeal to him. "What do we sell? Black slaves? Objects of religious significance? Cursed stones?"

Claude sighed. "All right, you're a poet," he said. "I don't understand why poets can't make the effort to get along like everyone else."

"Ah," Robert said. "But we poets can't understand why everyone else is making the effort."

"Because it's civilized, that's why," Claude said. His voice did not change. "Because our civilization depends on it."

"And where did that get us?" Robert said. Why am I the only one in our family who ever gets angry? he thought. "Four years of insanity, of madness in the trenches—that's what your civilization leads to." He thought of the people in the future—thousands and thousands of them—who had decided not to go along any more. He thought of Solange, who would understand everything he had said to Claude and everything he wanted to say. At least he knew he wasn't alone.

"I didn't want to discuss politics with you," Claude said. "I just—"

"I wasn't discussing politics—"

"—just wanted to ask if you'd like a job. Now I'm beginning to regret making the offer."

"You don't have to regret it," Robert said. "I wouldn't take it anyway."

"Fine," Claude said. "What are you going to do with your life? Sell poems?"

Robert looked past his feet and grinned at him. "Sell liquor to the Americans," he said. "And this time—" he took his feet off the desk— "I'm going to leave the room first. Good day." He stood up and left the library.

Claude did not speak to him until the next day, when he offered to loan him a suit and shoes for the funeral. Robert, still hung over from drinking and gambling the night before with Georges, dutifully put on the suit. As the family made their way to the black car parked at the curb his mother said, "Claude, I thought I told you to get him some better shoes."

"I did, Mother," Claude said.

"They were far too big," Robert said. "There's nothing wrong with these shoes."

"Nothing wrong—" Madame St. Onge said. "There's a hole in that one, can't you see it? Oh, never mind. Put your feet under the pew and hope no one will notice."

Claude opened the back door for his mother and sat beside her. "I suppose we sit up front," Noelle whispered to Robert. She looked very pale in her black dress. Her husband, standing beside her, seemed an almost intentional contrast, sandy-haired and florid-faced. For a moment Robert couldn't remember the man's name.

"Don't worry," Robert said. "I'll sit up front with the driver. You two can sit in back."

"There's not enough room," Noelle said. She was still whispering, as if the corpse parked a few cars back could hear her. In the end Noelle's husband sat in the back seat and Noelle and Robert sat up front.

No one spoke. Robert remembered very clearly saying to Georges the night before, "This will be the second time in a week I'll have been inside a church," and Georges saying, "Yes, and you'll probably sleep this time too." Lucky Georges was back at the casinos today.

Noelle stayed next to Robert all during the service. "Do you remember," she said, whispering above the priest's voice, "how he always said he'd take us to America?"

"Who did?" Robert said, half-listening.

"He did," Noelle said. She paused. "Father," she said.

"No, I—"

"He had all those maps up in the library," Noelle said. "I wonder if they're still there."

"I don't know," Robert said, trying to remember.

"And one year he even sent away for information

on sea voyages," Noelle said. She said the words "sea voyages" as though they had a special meaning for her alone. Her eyes, so dull in the car, began to shine. "He said that America was more interesting than France because in America they're still learning how to do things. Even though a lot of the things they've learned are wrong."

Robert sat in silence. That sounds fairly intelligent, he thought. I wonder why I never knew any of this. Maybe that's where I got my interest in American blues. I will never be able to talk to him about America, he thought, and suddenly, to his horror, he was crying. A piece of his past was gone, just like that. Damn, he thought. I wish I could have said good-bye.

Georges came in from the casinos the next morning at seven. "We've got to get out of here," Robert said, rolling over in bed and opening one eye.

"What?" Georges said, loosening his tie. "I thought you were asleep."

"I was," Robert said. "We've got to go back to Paris. Now."

"Right now?" Georges said. "Aren't you the one who usually sleeps till noon?"

"Listen," Robert said. He sat up, propping himself against the headboard. "My brother's busy getting ready to take over the entire estate. My sister's trying to drag me back to some wonderful childhood that never really existed. My mother doesn't like my shoes. If we leave now we'll be gone before they get up."

"Your—your brother?" Georges said. "But— Can he do that? I mean, isn't there a will?"

"I've been disowned," Robert said. "Disinherited. Cut off. It's time, they tell me, for me to grow up. Let's get back to Paris. I've got to live up to their expectations by acting irresponsibly again."

Georges shrugged. "All right," he said. "We can sleep on the way, I guess." He opened the valise and began picking up clothes.

Madame St. Onge met them at the front door. "Are you leaving?" she said. "I was hoping you'd stay a few days. You still haven't told me—well, your plans . . ."

Robert walked past her, carrying Georges's valise as proof of his intention to leave. Noelle came to the top of the stairs. "Good-bye, Noelle," he said. "I hope you get to take your sea voyage." He walked down the front pathway, threw the valise in the trunk of Georges's car and climbed over the door to the passenger seat.

He slept nearly the entire trip back. Snatches of strange dreams came to him—he was taking a train to America, was crossing the ocean . . . A dark man played a guitar. "Hard on you, losing your inheritance like that," Georges said once after he had been awake for a few minutes, dully watching the countryside.

"It is," Robert said, not wanting to talk but feeling that Georges deserved something. He managed to keep up a conversation for a while—the distance from Grenoble to Lyon—and then fell gratefully back asleep.

Georges dropped him off in front of his apartment. "Good-bye," Georges said. "Let me know how everything turns out."

"All right," Robert said. "And thanks. Thanks for the ride. Sorry it wasn't the vacation you wanted." Georges shrugged, honked the horn once and drove off.

Almost as soon as Robert got to his room he sat down and took out a piece of paper. "One by one the familiar patrons came into the café," he wrote. "The white-haired young man who never drank anything but milk. The old woman with the cat across her shoulders.

The fat man. The sixteen-year-old girl. They waited in the darkness. Then the dark-haired woman began to sing."

He stopped writing once to turn on the light when the room got dark, and once to go downstairs and buy cigarettes and groceries. He wrote the next day and the next, ignoring his friends, rarely leaving the room, covering sheets and sheets of paper.

He worked steadily. Some days he wrote without eating, and only noticed he was hungry when he stood up. Outside his room snow was coming down, transforming Paris with enigma and silence. Each tree stood stark and alone, each branch had its spectral double of snow.

In his mind and on paper the novel took shape. The main character was a woman, tall and dark-haired, the leader (somehow) of a group of street characters. The black letters formed the shape of her hair. The white paper was her body. Gradually he noticed he was writing two novels, the one on paper and the one in his head. In his mind he talked to Solange endlessly, about politics, art, love, revolution. She answered all his questions. He told her about his friends, his family. She agreed with him a hundred times. She marvelled at his subtlety, laughed at his jokes. They made love.

One day there was a knock at the door. He stood up wearily, trying to think how to get rid of the visitor. It was André, carrying papers.

"Hello, Robert," André said, closing the door behind him. His presence filled the room. "What have you been doing? We haven't seen you at the café for weeks."

"Writing," Robert said. He lit a cigarette.

"Writing? Writing what?"

"My novel."

"Your novel?" André said. "I thought you'd given up that idea."

"No," Robert said slowly. His mind was still back with his characters. Despite the jacket André had given him, he was cold. "I—I've been disowned."

"Georges told me," André said.

What else did he tell you? Robert thought. Did he tell you that my father died? Why can't you say anything to me? "No money," Robert said, shrugging. "So— it's time to go out into the real world."

"Absolutely not!" André said.

Robert smiled. This was the friend he remembered from years ago. "I agree," he said. "That's why I'm writing the novel. If it's published I won't have to go to work."

"Can I read it?" André said. "Here, wait. I brought you these," he said, handing Robert the papers under his arm. "The manifesto of surrealism. I wrote it last week. We're a movement now, with a name and a purpose. I can add your name to the others who have signed it."

Robert sat at the chair near the desk. André sat on the bed. They read in silence for a while. Robert's cigarette went out unnoticed. At last André looked up. " 'The blind flower-seller nodded,' " he read. " 'The pickpocket scratched his knees. The dark-haired woman looked at all of them remorselessly. "Don't you see?" she said. "This is the way it's got to be done." ' "

Robert looked at his friend, puzzled. "No, I'm sorry," André said. "This is unacceptable." He took the first page of the manuscript and tore it in half.

"What are you doing?" Robert said, alarmed. He grabbed the rest of the manuscript from André's hands as André tore the second page in half. "Stop that!"

"This is unacceptable," André said again. Only then

did Robert see how angry he was. "This is exactly the sort of thing I was talking about in the manifesto. A series of descriptions. A series of postcards! No, this is a disaster from beginning to end. It is stillborn, Robert. Bury it now."

"How dare you—" Robert said. His anger choked the words in his throat. "How dare you tear up my manuscript? How dare you come into my room—come into my room uninvited—and tell me that there is only one way to write, and that's your way? That everything else should be destroyed, buried, forgotten?"

"Surely you can't be proud of this—this catalog? Write a poem. Write a letter to the President or to Buster Keaton. Anything would be better than this. The only way I could publish this travesty would be as an example of what to avoid."

"Get out," Robert said. "Who asked you to publish it?"

"I—" André said.

"Get out," Robert said. "I don't ever want to see you again. I'm busy writing what I want to write—what you kept me from writing for seven years. If I never see you again my life will have taken a turn for the better."

"Fine," André said. "Fine. Don't expect to come around to the café. As of this moment you're no longer in the movement. I've never made such a bad mistake in judgment in my life as the day I told you my theories for the first time. The fortune-teller at the flea market was right—I've been disappointed by a friend. By my oldest friend."

"Don't call me your friend," Robert said. "You know why I didn't feel anything when I heard my father died? Because I already had someone in line for the job. You've always wanted to be my father, my teacher, my priest—anything but my friend. So go ahead—

excommunicate me. But when all your so-called friends are driven away don't come back to me. I have better things to do."

"Of course you do," André said. "You have to write trash that will be brought out by the most simple-minded publisher in Paris. You're right—you'll probably be able to make your living writing. The fools in Paris outnumber the chimney pots."

He slammed the door behind him. Robert, still shaking, could not think of anything to shout after him to sum up seven years of friendship. He sat on the edge of the bed, still holding the manifesto in his hand. Outside his window the weak winter sun went down behind a clutter of houses. He did not move for a long time. What have I done? he thought. What have I done?

FIVE

" 'Transform the world,' Marx said; 'Change life,' Rimbaud said—these two watchwords are for us one and the same."

André Breton

Robert leaned back in his chair and stretched until his shoulders cracked. It was a week after André's visit and enough of the book was written for him to see where it was going. As he turned back to the page he heard the sound of something rustling, and looked around in time to see a piece of paper being pushed under the door. He sighed. The chapter was nearly finished. He stood and went to the door to pick it up.

"It is not enough to sit in cafés drinking grenadine and speaking marvelous nonsense," he read. André's beautifully clear handwriting was unmistakable. "If surrealism is a game then it is a game being played for high stakes, and played all over the world. A certain commitment, not of a few hours, or a few poems, or a few jokes, but a commitment *for life* . . ." He read on. André had meant what he had said, then, he thought, a little numb. He was being expelled from the movement.

Only then did he think to open the door, but André was of course long gone. How does he get past the concierge? Robert wondered, remembering suddenly Antonin's description of André as a "true magus." No, that was ridiculous. He looked back at the document in his hand, wondering what to do next.

The walls of his apartment were suddenly too close. The door still stood open: Paris requested his appearance at a thousand new and old discoveries. He took his jacket from the back of the chair and went downstairs for his first walk in nearly a month.

Paris lay mantled in snow, silent, white, untrodden. Once again the world had changed completely by the act of turning a corner. He chose a road at random—objective chance, André said inside his head—and set off.

Everyone is gone, he thought, lighting a cigarette and throwing the match into the snow. The silence was oppressive. My life is as featureless as this landscape. My father is gone forever. The rest of the family—it might as well be forever. They'll probably never speak to me again. I haven't seen Hélène for a month—I wonder who she's taken up with. And Solange, he thought. His mouth twisted. No, Solange was a dream.

He passed the opera and pulled his coat tighter around him. And what was happening to André and the others? There's a story I'll never get to the end of, he thought. I'll never see any of those people again either.

Not that I mind, he thought defiantly. It's about time I left them, time I grew up. About time I started doing my own work, instead of standing in André's shadow. I wonder how many critics will call my book "surreal" when they review it. Well the hell with them. The hell with everyone. I'll horsewhip them if they do, the way Louis keeps threatening to if anyone reviews his books. Funny how I keep thinking about that group. Maybe I still miss them a bit. But that'll pass. I'll meet new people.

He looked around. The Tuileries Gardens were ahead of him and he walked inside, brushing past trees and statues. Soft snow was falling around him. The statues look cold, he thought. Someone should give them fur coats for the winter. He looked down the main path for a bench and saw her once again. Solange.

This time he was more angry than surprised. The undercurrent of anger that had started with André's excommunication and continued to include everyone who had deserted him welled up within him now. He walked over and sat on the bench next to her.

"Hello," she said. He had forgotten how musical her voice was.

"What do we do now?" he said harshly. He ignored her nearness, her voice, her hair. "Do you tell me you don't have enough time for me and run away while I stand around and look like a damn fool? We could do that again if you like. I've gotten pretty good at it."

"I'm sorry," she said.

"You're sorry," he said, not letting her continue. "That's good—I'm glad you've got feelings about something. Have you any idea what's been happening to me while you've been gone? My entire life has changed.

I've spent the last hour wondering if I was the last person left on earth. Sometimes I feel as though I am."

"I'm sorry," she said again. "I didn't know you would show up when you did the last time. Time is in flux—we can't always control what's happening. But we've learned a little more about things since then. I should—" she stopped, drew a long breath—"I should be here for a while. So you can ask me questions now. If you want to," she said almost shyly.

"If I want to!" he said, exploding. All his anger was leaving him, and he thought it was unfair because he didn't think she should get off that easily. "If I want to. Do you know I've thought of nothing but you for— sometimes for days at a time?" He stammered a little, remembering some of the things he had imagined them doing together. "I guess—I guess I'm in love with you. It's ridiculous, I know," he said, talking quickly, hoping to keep her from interrupting with explanations. "I've only seen you twice. Three times now. And I have the photograph. I can't explain it—it's never happened to me before. And I don't even know your name!" He stopped. He had the feeling that he had been babbling nonsense.

"Solange," she said. He watched her face closely, wishing he could read her expression, thinking that somehow he had mislaid or never found the key to her moods: hope and anticipation and apprehension and— Was it happiness? Had his words made her happy?

"Solange," he said, trying to collect his thoughts, to be rational. "All right. I guess I should hear your story, who you are, where you come from. I— Hell, I don't even know where to start asking questions. Tell me something, anything. What day were you born?"

"May twenty-first," she said. "Nineteen forty-nine."

He raised his eyebrows. "I *thought* so," he said softly. "From the future. But how?"

"We don't really know," she said. He looked at her again. This was the first time he had seen her sitting still, and it seemed wrong somehow. She should be in motion. All her excitement and momentum had concentrated in her eyes, which seemed to give off sparks, and in her hands. "The revolt—it's a rebellion against everything. We're freeing something—something we didn't even know was in chains. Dreams, madness. Even restrictions on time. Have you ever thought— have you ever wondered why time flows only one way?"

"Yes," he said. "Why does it?"

"I don't know," she said. "But why should it? We're asking questions now, not just questions of professors and presidents but of the universe itself. We've opened up something inside ourselves, something new. We want to change everything," she said forcefully.

"And so you discovered you could walk through time," he said.

"Yes," she said. "When the conditions are right you can walk through time. It has to do with dreams—I think I could explain it to you if I had enough time. We realized we needed help, and we thought we could get that help from the past. And we thought that the surrealists, since they were the closest to us in spirit, could help us the most." Her eyes shone as she spoke. Now that he knew her age he realized that she was much younger than he had first thought her. "And we chose you—well, I chose you, because I could go through time the easiest. I chose you because you have the best sense of humor." She looked at him then, with great energy and defiance, almost daring him to tell her that that was a terrible way to make a choice.

He laughed. "I'm sorry," he said, delighted that he

had been the one chosen. "I wish I could help you. I—I'm thrown out. Excommunicated. I'm not a surrealist any more."

"Well, we knew that would happen," she said. "You see—we'd read the history books."

He shivered. Someone is walking over my grave, he thought. He felt as he had in the future, out of place, thrown out of time. He had only to ask her about those history books and he would *know*. . . . "Why did you contact me, then?" he asked, trying to dispel his dark thoughts. "I haven't been to the café in over a month."

"I'd like to ask you to go back," she said.

"To go— No. No, I don't think so," he said. "My freedom means a lot to me. Did you really think I'd go back just because you asked me to?"

"I hoped so," she said, her hands stilled for once. "I think you will."

"You think," he said, trying to sort out past and future tenses. "Or the history books say. Which one is it?"

She shook her head. "The history books don't say anything about this part of your life," she said. "We think you'll go back when I tell you our story."

"All right," he said. "Tell me. Tell me about yourself."

"First we had to figure out how to reach you," she said as if beginning a fairy tale. "It was my idea to sell you the record at the flea market. I know you collected American blues artists."

"You knew—" he said. He tried not to let his astonishment show. How much more did they know about him?

"So I asked a friend of mine, a man from Spain, to leave the record on the table," Solange said.

"The man with the accent!" he said. "I remember him now."

"And then you went and left the record in the café—"

"—so you had to return it to me, at the Bureau of Surrealistic Research," he said. "But why—why is it broken?"

"It isn't," she said. "It can be played. You can play it in the future."

"But why—" he said, feeling trapped. He wanted to scream. Every answer led only to another question.

"It has to do with the way records are made," she said. "The grooves are closer together on our records— you couldn't play them on your machines. But we didn't realize that until later." She laughed. "I think it worked out anyway. It certainly got you curious enough."

"Frustrated enough, certainly," he said.

"I'm sorry," she said again, but this time her eyes sparkled.

"And the fortune-teller at the flea market?" he asked.

"She wasn't one of us," Solange said. "I don't know how she knew. We don't know—there's so much we don't know. None of us are scientists. Well, some of us studied science at the Sorbonne, before—before everything changed. But this isn't a science you can study anywhere. I don't even know what it would be called."

He must have looked uncertain, because she went on. "For instance— Well, the day we contacted you, the day we came to the past, your clock stopped. It stopped at a quarter to one." Robert nodded. He was beyond amazement now, someplace where marvels happened as regularly as dandelions. "Years from now a surrealist named Magritte will paint a picture of a locomotive coming out of a fireplace. The painting is—will be—called 'Time Transfixed.' And the clock on the mantel above the fireplace is stopped at a quarter to one."

He realized he had been holding his breath and let it out. "Why?" he asked.

"I don't know," Solange said. "Your friend Breton is right. Not everything has a rational explanation."

"All right," Robert said, then, belatedly, "He's not my friend. But what do you want from me? Why have you studied my life so closely? You seem to know more about me than I know myself."

Solange laughed. "It's not that difficult," she said. "You've written—will write—quite a bit about yourself. And the reason I read it all—well, one of the reasons—is that we need your help."

"My help?" Robert said. "But what can I do? I couldn't do anything the two times I was there."

"We wanted to show you—well, to show you what we believe in, how we live. To get your approval."

"Well," Robert said. He felt on familiar ground again. This was how one of his imagined conversations had gone. "What do you believe, then? I should tell you, I guess—I don't believe in anything. Not in any system like communism or capitalism. Life's too strange to fit into any system. I just want—"

"—to have a good time," Solange said. "I know. I know a lot about the surrealists by now. Something one of my professors said last year—I don't even remember what it was. A quote of Breton's, maybe. I was fascinated. I went to the library and read almost everything they had on the subject. And I read about you—" For the first time he thought she looked embarrassed, but even that emotion was mixed with others: defiance, laughter. He studied her bright red winter coat, trying not to embarrass her further, hoping she'd go on.

"Well, I thought you were interesting." She still couldn't meet his eyes. "This whole thing—this whole project—was my idea. As if I had enough time to take on another project!" She laughed. "But I'd always wanted to meet the surrealists. Especially you." She looked up at him then. "See, everything I'd read about you—I was sure you were a revolutionary and didn't realize it. You say you don't believe in communism or capitalism. But neither do we. We're anarchists, if you want something to call us. But that's too simple, really. What we want—what all of us are working for—is an end to politics. An end to divisions. All of us free to pursue our own desires."

"That's easy to say," he said. "I don't see how you're going to do it."

"You can do it if everyone wants to do it," she said. "That's the point we're at now. Everyone's joining the strike. They're all saying no to the powers in control. It's sort of a quantum leap"—he looked briefly confused and she searched for another word—"a giant change in people's ways of thinking. Everyone knows these things. You just have to point it out to them that they know them."

"And you need my help to tell them this." Robert shook his head. "I've been trying to tell them all my life," he said. "Look, I said. The world could be a vastly different and wonderful place. Everybody change drinks, change clothes, change beliefs, change lives. I wanted to shake them up, to hasten coincidences. If that's being revolutionary then in my own small solitary way I was a revolutionary. Without a following, following nobody. The only thing it ever did for me was get me disinherited. I'm tired. Here it is, 1924—"

"Twenty-five," Solange said.

"What?"

"It's 1925," she said. "You missed New Year's Day."

"You see?" he said. "My life slides away from me. I should have done something by now, should have accomplished something. All I've accomplished so far is that I've stayed a child forever."

"But that's a wonderful achievement," she said. "That's one of the things I admired about you. Growing up seems terribly overrated to me."

"I know," he said. "I used to think when I was younger that becoming an adult was something like dying. You'd achieved stasis. Doing the same things with the same people at the same times . . . I still feel like that. I feel that, strange as it sounds, staying in André's group for so long was a sort of stasis. But I want to do something. I want to write a novel. I don't suppose you people approve of the novel either."

"Not really," she said. "Most of us think it's a dead art form."

"So there you are," he said. "Why couldn't you have left me alone, left me to write my novel in peace? You can't ask me to fight a revolution I don't believe in. All day I've been thinking that life is empty, featureless, static. You go back to your spring and let me stay here in winter. I can't do anything to help you." Why was he saying these things? Did he just want to keep her talking? He couldn't feel that life was empty when it was filled with marvelous meetings like this one. He was almost ready to go wherever she asked, to fight a fantastic surrealistic revolution for her sake.

"I'm not just asking you, Robert," she said. He shivered. He had known that there would be more, had known that she wouldn't leave so easily. "I'm—well, we're desperate. Things have gone bad. We—we need you."

"Why?" he asked. "How?"

"The president made a speech on television," she said. He looked blank again and she said, "Television. Well . . ." She laughed. He shrugged and laughed with her. "He made a speech, anyway. Things are turning in his favor. Half a million people marched in support of him that night."

He nodded to show he understood. "And it's not just that," she said. "It's— Do you remember the people on stage at the demonstration? The—the jugglers?"

He nodded again. "I was wondering about them," he said.

"They're from my group," she said. "Some of them, and some of them were just people at the demonstration. They've managed to open the way into—I don't know what you'd call it. Into some other realm. The realm of dreams, maybe. They keep the avenues of time open, anyway. And that thing—that thing that appeared at the end—" She shuddered. It was the first time he'd seen her look afraid. "It's discovered the avenues too. I don't know where it's from. Maybe it's something from all of our dreams, from our nightmares of power and domination. It's gaining control. One person—one person has already been found with his throat ripped out."

"That could be anyone," he said, unwilling to face his memories of the man in the mask. "That could have been the police."

"It looked like—it looked like claws," she said, so softly he wasn't sure he'd heard her right. "We don't— none of us know what to do."

"Why ask me, though?" he said. "I don't even know what television is." He pronounced it slightly wrong and she laughed for a moment, easing the tension around her mouth and eyes. He decided he wanted to make her laugh more often.

"Well, we thought—the surrealists might be able to come up with something. You know about dreams, the unconscious. Even if you don't know what the creature is—"

"No, I don't," he said.

"—you might come up with a new idea, something we hadn't thought of. That's one of the things I liked about the surrealists—they were probably the most creative force of their time."

"We are?" Robert asked, surprised. He had just thought of the café meetings as a place to go at night.

"Yes, you are," she said, nodding. She saw his doubt and nodded again. "Really."

"Wait a minute," he said. "Here's a creative idea for you. Why don't you just go ahead into the future—your future—and see how the whole thing turns out?"

She laughed again. Much better, he thought. "We tried that," she said. "We can't get to the future. We don't know why."

"I can," he said.

"You need a guide, someone to bring you there," she said. "I brought you forward the two times you went, though I'm not really sure how I did it the second time. And I'll bring you again, if you want to go."

He hesitated. He badly wanted to light a cigarette, but something told him she wouldn't like it. "We need you," she said. She looked at him with the intensity of burning wire. "You and your friends might be the ones to make the difference—the difference between winning or losing everything."

"How can I go?" he said, wanting to be convinced, thawing despite the cold. "I don't believe in politics. In causes. Not even yours."

"But we don't believe in causes either," she said.

Her face was drawn, tight. "Don't you see? We want the same things. But you want them just for yourself, and we—we want them for everybody."

That's true, I do, he almost said. What's wrong with that? But he stopped himself. He found himself listening to her voice and wondering again what she sounded like when she sang. He felt the need in him, strong as hunger, to hear the record she had left for him. His heart rose. He would follow her to the future, follow his destiny, change his life, begin adventures again. "All right," he said. "I'll do it. But not because I believe in your politics. I'll do it because it sounds like fun."

"I thought so," she said. She was smiling. The tension had left her face, this time, it seemed, for good. "That's another reason I picked you."

"And—I won't lie to you—I want to see you again. But I can't—you can't ask me to talk to André. I can't go see him again. There's too much pride, broken promises, tangled friendships—"

"But we need him too," she said. "We need both of you."

"Fine," he said, angry now. What did she want with André? He felt used, a means to an end. "Why did you bother to ask me, then? Why did you decide to talk to me at exactly the point I've stopped seeing him? I've told you—I can't go talk to him. We'll never speak to each other again."

"I was hoping you'd change your mind," she said. "I was hoping your friendship would overcome everything."

"Well, it won't," he said. "You go talk to him yourself. Send him forward in time—see what he thinks of a real revolution. I'm going to go back to work now." He stood up, fishing in his pocket for a cigarette. He would substitute her beliefs for his own half-formed feelings, he would drop his writing, his life for her and her cause, but this was the one thing he would not do. He would not—could not—talk to André again. If she asked him this then despite his love for her, despite the way his heart rose whenever he saw her, he would never see her again. He would cut her off the way he had cut off everyone else, his family and his friends.

"Wait," she said. "Please. We need you in this— somehow I know we do. You and André both. Please talk to him."

He shrugged and lit the cigarette. His fingers were shaking. "I've told you—I can't," he said. "Really—you should go to the café yourself if you think he's that important. I've told him a little about you—he'd probably be interested to meet you. I've got to go now."

He turned and walked away from her. He couldn't resist a last backward glance. "Good-bye," she said. "I'll see you again."

He wondered if that was true. Perhaps she knew something that he didn't. He hoped so, fervently. He didn't think he could bear a life without her, a life where all the colors had run out. She gave him the excitement he had found before with André and his friends. But why was she making impossible demands of him? Why couldn't she accept him for what he was, accept the fact that his friendship with André was over? He stopped himself before he could become too angry with her. But a part of him still resented her for her mysterious appearances and disappearances, for the way she had made him love her.

He walked slowly back to his apartment. The snow had stopped. He realized that he was almost warm, that the heat of the argument had warmed him. It looked as though the sun would come out some time that day.

He wrote steadily for the rest of the week, taking a break once to hear Sidney Bechet at a café on Montparnasse. He avoided the place where Hélène worked. What could I tell her? he thought. That a part of my life has ended? He imagined her going to work steadily and coming home, forgetting about him, perhaps finding someone else. My problems have nothing to do with her, he thought. Maybe I'll see her later, when I get everything worked out.

He got back to his apartment late, around four in the morning. He had spent most of the night telling everyone where he'd been and denying the wild rumors that had sprung up in his absence. Defiantly he made as much noise as he could climbing the stairs. The concierge had been getting complacent lately. In the dark he fumbled for the doorknob and opened his door.

Someone was sitting on the bed, holding something. In the glare of the light—who had turned it on? he wondered—he could only make out that it was not a woman. He blinked a few times. "Hello," André said.

"Hello," Robert said stupidly. "How did you get past the concierge?"

"She knows I'm a friend of yours," André said. "She says you haven't paid your rent for January yet. Is that the first thing you have to say to me?"

"I'm tired," Robert said. "I don't really want you in my room, if you want to know the truth. Did you tear up anything while I was gone? No, everything looks— What the hell is that?" he said, noticing for the first time the object André was holding in his lap.

"I went back to the flea market," André said. "I wanted to see if the woman was still there—the fortune-teller, the one who had predicted such great things for you."

"And was she?" Robert said, interested in spite of himself. It's going to be a long night, he thought wearily, and sat down in the chair.

"No," André said. "But I found this." He held up the object. It was a wooden box containing a spring, some kind of mechanism, a few feathers and a blue goblet holding a globe. The box had been papered with stars.

"What is it?" Robert asked.

"A found object," André said.

"Yes but—" Robert said.

"I don't know," André said. "It's intriguing. It has no function, or if it does, its function is to make you think all sorts of thoughts you can't describe. It's an object from dreams."

"Where did you find it?" Robert said, beginning to wake up.

"At the flea market, I told—"

"Yes, but where at the flea market?" Robert asked. "It has a purpose, all right. I think I know what it is."

"Near where the fortune-teller was," André said. "I don't really remember. What is it? It was on a table with some women's fans and gloves—"

"And phonograph recordings?" Robert asked.

"I don't— Wait. There was a phonograph player there, I remember that. Probably some recordings too. Why? How do you know?"

They had taken his advice and contacted André, hooked him with an object significant only to him. André was about to embark on a voyage of adventure and leave him behind, and all because of a stupid quarrel. . . . No. He closed his eyes, trying to think. It wasn't a stupid quarrel, it had been his fight for freedom, for independence. "Robert?" André said, sounding far away. He opened his eyes. "What were you going to say? Don't go to sleep."

"I'm tired," Robert said. "Let me go to sleep. Let me think about it. I'll tell you later."

"You can't—" André said.

"Yes, I can," Robert said. "You remember the last time you talked to me you told me you never wanted to see me again." He said it without anger, almost as though remembering something that had happened thirty years ago. "Please. I'll talk to you later. At the café. Good night."

"All right," André said. He stood up, holding his found object carefully. "At the café tomorrow."

I didn't say anything about tomorrow, Robert thought, but he nodded to André as André let himself out.

He could not write at all the next day. It was unfair of them to have contacted André, to have preferred André to him. It was perfectly fair—after all, he had suggested it to them himself. His mind refused to hold the same opinion twice. He would never see André again. He would tell Solange to forget about the surrealists and go back to the future. He would meet André at the café and they would go into the future together. At about three or four in the afternoon he heard a knock on his door.

"Hello," the concierge said, puffing from the climb to his apartment.

"Hello," he said. He turned down the phonograph player.

"You probably think—" she said. She paused to get her breath back. "That I don't know anything. That I'm completely ignorant of what goes on around here."

"What do you mean?" Robert said.

"I know people, you know," the concierge said.

Robert wondered how old she was. She seemed to have been born stout. "I hear what goes on, especially when it concerns my house. Never mind who told me, but I found out who that visitor was you had last night. A friend of yours, he said he was." She laughed mirthlessly.

"Who was he?" Robert asked.

She looked at him suspiciously, trying to decide if she was being mocked. "André Breton, that's who he was," she said. "The one who's going around saying all those terrible things about France. If he comes back here— Don't you laugh at me! I've met a lot of young men like you, ungrateful for everything we've done for them in the war."

"I'm very grateful," Robert said, leaning against the doorjamb. "I probably couldn't have afforded to see Germany by myself."

"Don't laugh!" she said. "You tell your friend André that he's not welcome in my house. And if you knew half the things he's done you wouldn't want him here either. Charging into fancy dinners shouting, 'Long live Germany,' swinging from chandeliers—"

That was me, Robert thought. I swung from the chandelier. He said nothing.

"And now I hear he's written a manifesto," the concierge said. "A manifesto, you hear? Probably about overthrowing the government, letting those Germans right back in. You tell him he's not welcome here. And another thing—"

Robert had turned to go. "Yes," he said, coming back.

"The landlady says you haven't paid your rent for January," she said.

"Oh?" he said. "Is it January?"

The concierge ignored him. "She might have let you go a few weeks, but I've been telling her some things about you and your friends." I'll bet you have, Robert thought. "You have until the end of the week."

"And then what?" he said. "We just forget the whole thing?"

"And then we throw you out, M. St. Onge," she said. "Don't think other people wouldn't want to live in your apartment." She looked around the one room doubtfully. "I can understand if you have family problems," she said shrewdly. "Perhaps we can work something out."

"I have no family problems," he said. He was damned if he would give her the satisfaction of prying into his affairs. "I have no family."

She shrugged and turned to go. "Till the end of the week then," she said.

He turned the phonograph player up as loud as it would go. That was it then. He was trapped. Come up with the money by the end of the week or go work for his mother and brother. He turned off the phonograph abruptly. Or go into the future. He took the jacket off the back of the chair and went outside.

André sat alone inside the café. He looked a little nervous, as if he had thought Robert would not show up. "Hello," he said as Robert sat down.

"Hello," Robert said. A sudden awkwardness came between them. "How—how are you?"

"Yes," André said, as if that were a possible answer to the question. He sipped his drink. "What do you know about the object I found at the flea market? And how did you find out?"

"Do you remember the recording I bought the last time I was there?" Robert said. "The one I left at the café, the one that was returned to the Bureau?"

"Yes, of course," André said. "The one you wrote

about." His eyes widened slightly. "What you wrote—it was true, right? I remember you told me."

"That's right," Robert said. He felt a small moment of triumph. This was as close as André would come to an apology. "The woman from the future—Solange. She contacted me again yesterday." And he told André the rest of the story.

André looked as startled as he had ever seen him when he had finished. "From the future?" André said. "And—and they remember us?"

"Yes," Robert said, a little surprised. André had never doubted before that he would be remembered.

"And they want us to go with them?" André said.

"Yes," Robert said again. "They want both of us."

"But why you, though?" André said. "You're not a surrealist."

"I don't know," Robert said. He grinned. "I have a good sense of humor."

"I don't—I don't know," André said. He had never looked so uncertain. "Of course I'll go. But to go with you— It means compromising my principles. I've never compromised."

"I know," Robert said. "That's what they said about you in the future. But can't you just think of me as your friend? Not as a surrealist?" He found he was holding his breath waiting for the answer.

"You've rejected surrealism entirely then?" André asked.

"In my writing," Robert said. "I can't sign your manifesto. But not in my life."

"Your writing and your life are the same thing," André said. "To make a distinction between life and art is—"

"Don't lecture me," Robert said quietly.

"What?"

"Don't lecture me. I'm not a surrealist any more. I know what you're going to say, anyway. I don't need to hear it again."

"I'm not lecturing you," André said. "I'm trying to save you from making an important mistake—" Robert stood up. "All right," André said. He hesitated, thinking. "They need us in the future, is that what you said?" Robert nodded warily. He sat down. "We'll have to join together then. Put aside our differences of opinion. For now," he said, emphasizing the last two words. "After this thing is over—well, I don't know. We'll see."

"All right," Robert said, pleased. "Good. I'll try to find Solange and tell her what you've decided."

A few of the others came into the cafe. "Robert!" Louis said. "Where the hell were you? We'd heard you were—" He stopped and looked at André. "Well, anyway, welcome back."

"I was busy," Robert said. "Writing."

"Hello, Robert!" someone else said. "It's good to see you. Have you— Are you back with us?"

"For now," Robert said. He looked over at André. Why didn't anyone mention the excommunication? Were they that afraid of André?

The conversation drifted along familiar patterns. Word games, questions and answers, mad speculation, disturbing phrases. Several people asked Robert where he'd been and he gave them the same answer he'd given Louis. It was exciting to be back, exciting but frustrating. No matter where he went he would always end up in the same café with the same people hearing the same conversations, like Alice in *Through the Looking-Glass* trying to get to the garden of live flowers and always ending up at the house instead. He ordered a drink and sipped it slowly, watching. He itched to be somewhere else.

"Robert," Louis said, almost whispering.

"Yes?"

"André told me about your book," he said. Robert raised his eyebrows. "Don't worry—I haven't decided it's decadent trash. In fact—I think I may have a publisher. Someone mentioned to me that he's always liked your pieces in the magazine. Of course I'd have to read it first."

"Well—sure," Robert said, surprised. "I mean— Of course. I'd be glad to."

"And don't tell André," Louis said. "I'd be thrown out for good if he knew I was helping you."

Robert nodded. That was Louis all right, conciliatory to the point of holding two opposite opinions. "Of course," he said, wondering where all this intrigue was going to lead him. Still, what worse could André do to him? And a chance to be published—that was worth almost anything. "All right," he said. "I'll show you what I've written so far. Tomorrow."

The evening lengthened. The circus performers, like bright falling stars, shone briefly outside the window and were gone. The night's insistent lights came on. The conversation dazzled and bored by turns. He was a little drunk. Well I've done it, he thought. Together André and I will save the future. And he laughed.

SIX

"It is not the material advantage which each man may hope to derive from the Revolution which will dispose him to stake his life—his life—on the red card."

André Breton

Robert wadded up a twenty-franc note and, without looking, tossed it over to another table. Casually he glanced around, trying to see the person's reaction to the money falling from the skies. Surprise, delight, greed, even a little hostility. Robert laughed and tossed another note in another direction. It was a few nights later and Louis had come through with a publisher. Robert wondered how much of his advance he could spend in one night.

"That's the way to do it," said Jacques Rigaut,

sitting next to him. "Get rid of it now. You might be dead tomorrow."

"That's true," Robert said, throwing a note all the way across the café. "I'm aiming for that candle there in the middle of the table. What does money sound like when it burns? If I die my mother and brother will get it. I'd rather see it burn." He took another note out of his pocket, put it back. And if you don't die, he thought, and you waste it all tonight, you'll have to go to work in Nice. Don't listen to him. He's as mad in his own way as Antonin is.

"Nobody will get anything when I die," Jacques said. "I don't have anything. And I won't have anything in four years, either."

"You're sticking to your schedule then?" Robert asked. He had heard Jacques's story before but it still intrigued him. What would it be like to place yourself under a death sentence? André, he knew, was fascinated.

"Yes, I am," Jacques said. "In 1919 I gave myself ten years and I haven't seen anything since then to dissuade me. In fact it makes life easier, simpler. I make no plans for the future. I put nothing off until later. I haven't saved any money—I don't need it. If someone asks me what I want to do with my life I just say, 'Die.' "

"That's a stupid question anyway," Robert said. He's bluffing, he thought. He likes the attention. It's just a game he's playing. But he's been playing it for so long, about six years. "Have you got a date picked out?" he asked.

"Oh, yes," Jacques said. "Ten years to the day from when I first made my vow. I don't tell anyone what it is. I don't want anyone to stop me."

"Congratulations," someone said, sitting down at the table. "I hear you sold your novel."

"That's right," Robert said. "Want twenty francs?"

"I— No, thank you," the man said, glancing at André. A new one, Robert thought. I wonder who he is. Look at his nervousness—I bet he's wondering why a mere novelist is allowed in with the surrealists. That's the thing about André—no matter how many people he throws out, he can always find new ones to take their place. It's not his ideas, or not just his ideas. It's the force of his personality.

"Someone giving away money?" said another new person sitting across the table. "I could use some."

Robert took out a few notes and handed them across the table without looking at them. "Here you are," he said. "Don't spend it on anything serious."

"I— Thank you," the man said, surprised. "Thank you very much."

"A unicycle," Robert said. He hated being thanked. "Or a pet monkey. Something like that."

"A comb for your moustache," Louis said.

"A deck of tarot cards," André said.

Robert had stopped listening. Someone who looked very much like Solange was walking toward him through the dim light of the café, becoming clearer as she came. It was. It was she. "Hello, Solange," he said, unable to stop smiling.

"Hello," she said, sitting next to him and rubbing her hands. "It's so cold here. Where I— Where I come from we're already sitting outside the cafés." She was speaking only to him, but around the table conversation stopped as people turned to look at her. On his other side Jacques leaned back to see her better.

I hope there's not going to be trouble, Robert thought, suddenly worried. André always wants to be the center of attention. What is it about her? She's not pretty, not in the conventional sense. But she's beautiful. "André," he said, breaking into the conversation suddenly. "I want you to meet a friend of mine. This is Solange. Solange, this is André Breton." He felt very conscious that he didn't know her last name.

"Hello," Solange said. For the first time he saw her look shy. Could she be nervous about meeting André? What did he mean to her? André suddenly seemed to him as foreign as the people of her time.

"Hello," André said. "It's a pleasure to meet you."

"I feel the same about you," she said. "Robert's told you—he's told you my story?"

"Yes," André said. "I'm very interested. As anyone would be."

"And do you want to come?" she asked. "You once said, 'In matters of revolt, one should not need ancestors.' But you are our ancestors, and we do need you."

"Yes," André said again. His eyes were narrowed in concentration, studying what he had only heard about before. "Very much."

"Good," she said. She pitched her voice lower, so that by some trick only André and Robert heard her in the noisy café. "Please meet me tomorrow at noon in the Luxembourg Gardens. At the marionette theatre. I'll be waiting for you."

"Tomorrow," André said. "So soon?"

"Yes," she said. "It seems soon to you, but we have been waiting a long time. Do you want more time to prepare? We'll end up in the same place in the future no matter when we start."

André looked briefly confused. Robert, almost used to the changes in time, tried not to look pleased. For once he would be the leader, and André the follower. "Too soon?" André said. "No, not really. I have no commitments. One must always be ready for the great adventure."

Solange smiled. "Robert said almost the same thing," she said. "I can see why you two are friends."

André looked uncomfortable. Robert loved her more than ever at that moment. "Tomorrow then," she said. "At the Gardens."

"Are you leaving?" Robert said. There had been finality in her voice.

"I should," she said. "It's becoming harder and harder to keep the avenues of time open." She looked around. "The hell with it," she said finally. "If they think I'm going to miss a chance to drink with the surrealists they're crazy. What are you having? I'll have some of that. You'll have to pay for it—I don't think my money's good here."

Robert laughed, pleased that he had money to offer her. For the first time he dared to lean back and put his arm around her shoulder. "Of course," he said. He picked up his glass and saluted her. "To the future," he said.

Solange came hurrying inside the gates of the Luxembourg Gardens. "Come on," she said to them. Her voice sounded hoarse: Robert wondered what she had been doing since she left the night before. He hoped she was not going to ruin her singing voice. "This way."

She struck fire from their bones and sinews. They followed her without question, hurrying through the pale winter sunlight as though their lives depended on it. They went outside the park and rounded a corner. The familiar smell of gunpowder was tangled up in the spring air.

"Come on," Solange said again. André had stopped to look at the streets—the overturned cars, the torn up paving stones, the broken windows. Robert stopped too. Something was different. There were fewer people perhaps, or—no, that wasn't it—the people looked different. The joy was gone from their faces—they seemed grim now, grim and determined.

But otherwise everything was the same: the high buildings of steel and glass, the small cars, the street signs, many of them painted over, advertising strange and undreamed-of products. Robert felt as he had the first time he had entered a nightclub, driven by the need to hear the music. Then too everything had been strange and familiar at once. Gradually he noticed that all the nightclub patrons acted as though they had been there a thousand times before. And he did, too, surrendering himself to the place, the time and the music.

"Come on," he said to André. "You have to keep moving." He wasn't sure what he meant by that but André seemed to understand. They passed buildings covered with graffiti, buildings burned out or marked by bulletholes. No cars were running—perhaps the gas supply had given out. I wonder what André makes of all this, Robert thought. I wonder if I looked that slow-witted when I first came here. Probably I did.

They came finally to the Théâtre de l'Odéon. Solange pushed the doors open. Everything was dark, so dark that at first Robert thought they were about to show a film. He could feel rather than see people sitting all around him, filling the theatre.

Suddenly someone broke the silence. A voice—Robert couldn't tell if it belonged to a man or a woman—began to howl, climbing several octaves before stopping. Someone else from a different part of the room said simply, "He is gone." Then there was silence.

Robert felt for Solange's hand in the dark. "He died," Solange said to him in a low voice that didn't carry past the two of them. For the first time Robert heard in that sentence a summary of a man's life. "One of our friends. He was shot."

Someone near them started to tell a story about the man who had died. What if this was the kind of funeral we had had for my father, Robert thought. What if my mother had said "He died" instead of— what did she say?— "He passed away." Maybe I wouldn't be floundering around like this. Maybe I wouldn't be so aimless. Or maybe I'm doomed to be aimless no matter what happens. Sometimes it seems that way.

The woman telling the story had stopped. Someone else started to sing a song and a few people near him joined in. It was a parody of a popular song and no one else, it seemed, knew the words. Robert looked at Solange, not daring to let go of her hand, but either she didn't know the words or she didn't choose to sing. When it ended a few people were laughing. Some were crying. The lights came on suddenly and he blinked. His tears turned the lights to prisms.

"What do we do now?" someone said.

"What can we do?" someone else said. "The army's outside Paris right now."

"Did you hear what they said about us? 'Spoiled children who don't know what else to do with their lives.' That's what they called us. We've got to go on, even die fighting, until they understand us. Until they join us."

"You die fighting, friend. I prefer to live."

The debates went on. Robert looked around, bored. Why had Solange called him here? More people than usual were sleeping. Suddenly he heard applause and looked up to see who was speaking. It was Patrice.

"Look," Robert said to Solange. "It's your friend."

She looked up. "Patrice has become very important in the movement," she said. "He's mentioned a lot in the papers as one of our leaders. He just calls himself a spokesman."

"What happened to Paul?" Robert asked.

A small line appeared between her eyebrows. Robert almost didn't want to hear her answer. "No one's seen Paul," she said. "I don't know what happened to him."

"And Gabrielle?" he asked, remembering the bitterness that had been revealed beneath her optimism when he had asked her about Paul.

"Oh, Gabrielle's fine," Solange said. She almost laughed. "She's taken up with Patrice, in fact. So there's one story that's had a happy ending."

"Good," Robert said. He felt pleased for her. She deserved happiness—Gabrielle with her long fine hair and her open expression, readable as a clear pool of water. He wondered if she still thought Patrice was a bit fanatic.

People came and went. Printing committees were formed, and committees to distribute food to the people of Paris. A group that made posters came and recruited a few people to help. Ways of dealing with the army were discussed.

At last Robert stretched his legs. "I'm hungry," he said. "Is there any place we can find food?"

"So am I," Solange said. "I hate to leave this place— I think something's going to happen at any moment. But I can't sit still any more. Let's go to a café."

"A café?" Robert said. "Are they open?"

"Of course," Solange said. She grinned. "You don't expect the cafés of Paris to close, do you? A few of them have stayed open, and some of them are sympathetic to us."

They got up to leave. Robert half-expected someone to call Solange back, to ask her to help in some way, but no one did. The revolution is dying, he thought. They're just going through the motions, waiting for the army or the police. And yet something was about to happen. Solange had mentioned it and he felt it in the air.

They turned down a small street to a café. "We can get some good food here, I think," Solange said. "This time I'll pay for both of you. Your money might be good here but it'll probably cause some comment."

"You can't—" Robert looked at her. "Women don't pay for men," he said finally.

"Of course they do," Solange said. "They do in my time, anyway. Don't worry about it."

Robert said nothing. What was he afraid of? That if she paid for herself she would be too independent, uncontrollable? But her independence was one of the things he liked best about her. He remembered that he had only dared to put his arm around her after he had paid for her drink, that he had stopped seeing Hélène as soon as his money ran out, as though there were some final and irrevocable equation between the two things. It was a new idea and he was always ready to welcome new ideas. But it still disturbed him. André was silent too for once. "I feel uncomfortable," he said at last.

"You'll get over it," she said, walking ahead of him into the café.

Once inside they had to take their food from the kitchen. Only the owner had stayed on to cook. "They're on strike," he said, shrugging. He did not seem to care very much. "Everyone. No, that's all right, I don't want your money."

"But—" Solange said.

"I don't want it, I said," the café owner said. "Let's say that I am sympathetic to your cause, despite being an owner and a bourgeois. That I believe in what you are doing." He was looking at André as he spoke. Who was André to this man? Robert wondered. What did André inspire in people? Once again his old friend seemed like a stranger.

"Well—thank you," Solange said. "Thank you very much."

They took their food to the tables outside and sat down. "Ah," Robert said. "Sun. That's why I came with you, you know. It's too cold back in my time."

Solange laughed. "I'm glad I could offer you something," she said. "Something besides tear gas and policemen."

"That man in the café must have pleased you," André said to her.

"He did," she said. "Sometimes I think— It seems as though everyone's deserting us. They've had their fun, their vacation, and now it's time to go back to work. A speech by the president, a few attacks from the police, and it's all over. In a month no one will even remember us."

"I can't believe that," André said. "After this I don't think anything will ever be the same again."

"Maybe not," Solange said. "Maybe we'll be the inspiration for someone else, just as you were for us. But years from now, not in any future I can see."

"Maybe—" Robert said. He hesitated, not wanting to disagree with her. "Maybe that's just the way people are. Maybe they need to work six days a week and complain about the boss on their day off. They can't imagine anything better. Your future would scare them. It wouldn't work."

"I don't—" Solange said, but André said, louder, "Are you saying people don't dream?"

"Of course they dream," Robert said. He sighed. How had he started on another argument with André? "But they don't want—they don't want to be free. They can't imagine it. Look at my mother. Look at my concierge—"

"Look at the man inside that café," André said.

"Look at the factory workers," Robert said. "Most of them want higher wages and a few hours more off a week." He turned to Solange. "Isn't that right?"

"Well—yes, some of them," she said. "But that's because they don't know anything better. They need to be educated—"

"If they could see the quality of life they'd have—" André said.

Then why is your revolution failing? Robert thought. But he found he didn't want to argue with either one of them. They were talking to each other now, about surrealism and revolution and, for some reason, Charlie Chaplin films. Robert sat back and watched them. Solange was imitating someone, telling a story, her long fine legs stretched out in front of her, her arms gesturing. One minute her face was that of an elegant woman giving orders, the next she was a student shouting slogans. André was as close to laughter as Robert had ever seen him—he wondered if Solange knew what a compliment this was.

Last night she had listened to the wandering talk of the surrealists and he had seen them through her eyes, fascinating and new. Every so often she had looked at him and laughed, as if they shared a private joke, and once her hand had covered his. He had said little, wondering what her life was like in the future, wondering what she felt for him. Why had she come back in time for him, why had she studied him among all the strong personalities of the surrealists? He had hoped she would stay. But deep in the night, at around one or two—he had stayed longer at the café because she was there—she had gotten up as if in response to a summons only she could hear. At his swift look she had said, "They can't keep the avenues open any longer. I'm sorry. I'll be back tomorrow." And then she was gone.

Now he watched her talking, expressions moving across her face like clouds. She seemed relaxed and refreshed for someone who kept such odd hours. Of course they all kept odd hours, and these hours were just odder than most. He laughed a little and she looked at him quickly, sharing another joke.

Someone familiar was walking across the street, past two sleeping figures in a courtyard. "Look," Robert said, interrupting André and Solange. "Who's that?"

Solange shaded her eyes against the sun. "I don't know," she said. "People sleep outdoors all the time now. The police are too busy to pay attention."

"No," Robert said. "That man walking. Who is he?" The man turned a corner and was lost to them. "I thought it was Paul."

"Paul?" Solange said, looking up sharply. "Why— why would he come back? I thought he'd given up on us."

"I don't know," Robert said. "You know him better than I do."

Solange sighed. "He's the kind of person who wants to lead. The kind that needs followers. You know." Robert nodded, wishing he had the courage to look at André. "That's not what the movement's about. We reach—we try to reach our decisions by consensus. So that everyone can say something. It's slow, but at least no one feels left out or powerless. Paul never understood that. I didn't realize it at the time, but he just saw the revolution as a chance to gain followers."

"Is that why you left him?" Robert asked, guessing. He hoped her confessional mood would last.

Solange looked at him startled. "How did you—"

Robert laughed. "Now it's your turn," he said. "How does it feel to have a stranger knowing things about your life?" He saw her expression, apology mixed with understanding, and took pity on her. "Gabrielle told me," he said.

She nodded. "Of course," she said. "I don't know why I left him. I was busy, busy with the revolution, and—and other things . . ." Robert wondered what she had been about to say next. "It wasn't that I didn't like him," she said thoughtfully. "I just never really paid that much attention. I guess he wanted me as a follower too."

They sat silently for a while, sipping cups of black coffee. No one moved. Robert thought that in front of him were the two people he cared about most in the world, and that one of them had said he never wanted to see him again and the other lived in such a faraway place she might as well be on another star. Still, for the moment they were together. He heard shouts and police sirens in the distance. The streets were almost empty. Robert felt fine.

They watched the sun go down behind the courtyard across the street, drowning the sleepers in shadow. "It's getting late," Solange said. "We should get back."

It was evening when they returned to the Odéon. People sat around in groups of four or five, saying little. Patrice, nearly hoarse, was talking to a group near the entrance. "Look," Robert said, pointing to someone sitting in shadow near the corner. "I was right. It's Paul."

"Where?" Solange said.

"Over there," Robert said. For a moment he was almost glad to see him again, the first man who had welcomed him to this fantastic and unexpected world. "Hello, Paul," he called.

"Hello," Paul said, coming toward them. He looked at Solange, hesitating, but said nothing.

"Hello, Paul," Solange said.

"I'm surprised you're still speaking to me," Paul said. "Or haven't your informants told you where I've been?" He sounded bitter. Is this what happens to people when their world falls apart? Robert wondered.

"Informants? No one's told me anything," Solange said.

"Well, that's interesting," Paul said. "That shows how important I am to you, anyway. You've probably read some of my articles, though. The ones where I explain how you've sold out."

"What—what do you mean?" Solange said. She stood still, uncertain. Robert felt embarrassed, as though he were watching something intensely private.

"You almost had it," Paul said. "Higher wages, better working conditions. But you couldn't accept that, no. You had to go for something more, some bizarre utopia that only you would be happy living in—"

"I can't believe I'm hearing this," Solange said. "After all the discussions we've had, all the things we've talked about—"

"I'm just facing facts," Paul said. "It's a fact that the police wouldn't be here now if you had agreed to negotiate with the government—"

"Government!" Solange said. She stood with her hands on her hips, facing him. He couldn't meet her glance. Her eyes seemed to wound him. "You've never faced a fact in your life. What is it, Paul? Are you jealous that Gabrielle's gone off with Patrice? Or is it me? Are you upset with me?"

"Don't give yourself that much credit," Paul said. "I haven't even missed you. I— I've been busy." He smiled briefly, then smiled again, more broadly this time, as though holding a secret too wonderful to contain.

"Really?" Solange said. She moved impatiently from one foot to the other. She looked ready to hit him or to dance with him, depending on what he would say next. "What have you been doing?"

"You'd like to know, wouldn't you?" Paul said. A police siren sounded, quite near. Another one joined in. "Why, what an entrance," he said sardonically. "Here they are now."

"You wouldn't—" Solange said furiously. "You wouldn't betray us to the police! Your own friends?"

The sirens drowned her out. The doors opened. "All right," someone said. "We're evacuating this place."

Someone else turned on a megaphone. "Everyone out," he said. "This is an illegal assembly. Everyone please leave now."

The police came through the open doors. "Paul—" Solange said threateningly. She took one step toward him.

"Watch out," André said suddenly. "They're coming for you. Someone must have tipped them off."

Solange jerked away from Paul. A few policemen were coming toward them. "Let's go," Robert said, amazed that he was able to think so quickly. "André, you go help Patrice. I'll stay here with Solange."

"All right," André said. He left just as a group of black-uniformed policemen reached them.

"You're under arrest," a policeman said. Robert

began to cough. "Tear gas!" someone said. Robert wiped his eyes—

The room seemed to expand, to contain more angles than were possible in geometry. The roof was lifting to reveal not dark night but a deep blue sky furrowed with stars. A comet went by. "Stop!" the policeman said from far away. "Stop moving! You're under—" the policeman coughed—"under arrest—"

The lights went out. Across the room Robert could see André's cane lit with a pale blue fire. He was leading Patrice somewhere, tracing an intricate pattern. Robert blinked, wiped his eyes again. André and Patrice were gone.

A darker light was coming from another part of the room. Robert turned, reluctant to face it. The man in the mask came on toward them slowly. He was out of proportion, huger than anyone near Robert. "No!" Robert said, almost screaming. He had never been as frightened. "No, go away! Go back! Solange, run!"

The man came closer, scattering people and chairs. "Wake up now," Robert said to himself, not caring who heard him. "Oh, please, wake up." He was almost whimpering.

"Solange," the man in the mask said. His voice sounded like rust, or like squeals. "Where is she?"

"She's gone," Robert said, trying to face his nightmare, hoping desperately that Solange had left. "She's not here."

"She's not?" said the man in the mask, taking his eyes off Robert for a moment. He looked back, fur and fang and metal leering. "Then you will come with me instead." His face grew nearer, blotted out the world. Then everything went black.

SEVEN

"Parents, tell your children your dreams!"
Surrealist Proverb

Robert woke. The room was dark, light enough only to see a few feet in front of him. The rest of the room seemed empty, but he couldn't tell. He stretched. Pain ran through one shoulder—he must have bruised it as he fell. Where was he?

A sound like machinery came from one end of the room, repetitious and endless. It had run through his sleep, he realized now, threading through uneasy dreams he could not remember. He could almost make out words in the droning sound, words and sentences. Fear leapt in his heart and he strained to see across the dim room. Was it he? Had they put him in this room with the man in the mask?

"—understandable, but wrong all the same," the man in the mask (or someone) was saying. "People don't want to work together, you see. Don't want to cooperate. Don't want to get along. That's our secret, you see. Our secret, but one that's been out in the open for thousands of years. They want a boss. They want a politician, a cop, a priest. They want—"

Robert screamed. The voice took no notice of him—the drone went on. Robert jumped to his feet, screaming hoarsely. He fell back, hitting the wall. He turned, hugging the wall. If he turned the corner there would be another corner, and if he turned that one there would be— No. He couldn't face it. He curled up against the wall. "—can't live with the sort of daily uncertainty you do," the voice was saying. Robert hugged his knees to his chest. Eventually he slept.

When he awoke the second time, everything was the same—the mechanical voice, the terrible light that was neither day nor night. "Everyone preys on everyone else," the voice was saying. Robert realized that it had continued while he was asleep, and wondered if the man in the mask ever slept. He shuddered. "The strong prey on the weak. The rich prey on the poor. The parents prey on their children." He felt hungry. His bladder was full and he turned and relieved himself in the corner.

"There will always be bosses," the voice said. "People will always want to be bosses. People will always want to have a little more than their neighbors—"

"I thought you said—" Robert said. His voice was hoarse. He cleared his throat and tried again. "I thought you said people always want bosses. How can they want bosses and want to be bosses at the same time?" He was trembling. It seemed to him that he had made a good point but at the same time he felt that he wasn't thinking clearly, that if only he could get out of the dreadful room he could argue better.

The voice had taken no notice of him. "That's where you were wrong, you see. That's where you made your mistake. People are always greedy for more. They will always want more than their neighbor has—"

"How can they want bosses and want to be bosses at the same time?" Robert said again, shouting. "How can they? You said something and I don't understand you. Explain what you meant. I didn't understand you."

The voice went on. Robert wondered if it was a recording. He didn't think it was. He felt some sort of presence there: the man (or whatever it was) had shifted a little while he slept.

"I don't want more than my neighbor," he said. "I don't want a boss, I don't want to be a boss. I'm perfectly willing to share! How do you explain that?"

The voice had continued speaking. Robert felt confused. Whose arguments was he presenting? He wasn't willing to share—what if everyone wanted to listen to his collection of blues recordings, for example? Who was he? Was he André, Solange, Hélène, his father?

Robert continued to shout at the voice for a few minutes, or a few hours. Time did not exist in the room. At last he leaned back against the wall to go to sleep. At least I'm catching up on my sleep here, he thought, and laughed. "At least I'm catching up on my sleep!" he shouted at the man across the room, hoping to stop him with humor. He had a feeling that his humor, like his logic, was better outside the room. The voice had not stopped.

Robert opened his eyes slowly. The light was the

same in front of his eyelids and behind them. He wondered why he bothered to open his eyes at all. "All right, all right!" he said loudly, trying to drown out the voice that had once again insinuated itself into his sleep.

"—how you could have believed all that rubbish," the voice said. "You seem intelligent, not like those friends of yours. You know you're not willing to band together with a group of people. You know you don't want to overthrow the system."

Robert stopped and listened. It was true, he didn't. "You know the system can't be overthrown," the voice said. Yes, that was true too. His presence here proved that.

"You've had your fun," the voice said. "Your childish experiments. But it's time to grow up now. Time to put away all of that. Time to go to work."

And do what? Robert thought. He ached for a cigarette. Work for my family in Nice? He felt almost ready to do that. The color, the music were slipping from his life just as they had slipped from this room. Why bother to have adventures? Why bother with surrealist games? Why bother to overthrow society when people would rather not have it overthrown? He could settle down and—well, maybe not get married, but have a house, and clothes, and a better phonograph player. . . .

He thought of Solange running through the streets of Paris, her long legs denying distances. Solange was alive. He thought of her speaking, her anger like fire. Solange was alive and he was dead, immured in this room thinking thoughts the dead think . . . "It was early, early one mornin'," he sang. His voice was terribly off-key. "When I heard my bulldog bark. Stagolee and Billy Lyons was squabblin' in the dark."

He sang all the way through "Stagolee," learned

from a recording of American folk songs, wondering if he had gotten the words right. He sang all the songs on his Bessie Smith recording and all the songs he had heard the black men and women sing in cafés on Montparnasse and Rue Pigalle. What a strange language American English was. What a strange place America must be, not the America on postcards and in books but the other one. Harlem. Gangsters. Shiny wide cars on quiet tires and people sitting by the road starving.

The voice paused for the merest second. Robert held his breath in hope. "You could be someone in society," the voice said. "With your skills and the backing of your family you could go far. You could—"

Robert laughed. It seemed to him that the voice had paused a little again. He knew now that he would never be anyone in society, that he would always be on the underside of whatever society there was. "If you catch me stealin', I don't mean no harm," he sang. "If you catch me stealin', I don't mean no harm. It's a mark in my family and it must be carried on."

For a long time he sat against the wall and sang. The singing almost covered the noise of the voice across the room and kept him from thinking about how hungry he was. After a time he lay down and slept.

He was hungrier still when he woke. He tried to figure how many days and nights he had gone without eating, but gave it up. How long was a day here? Was it the period between sleeps? Somehow he didn't think so.

At least, he thought, I've remembered a dream. I'll always remember this dream, the room and the voice and this strange light. Then he laughed. Was it a dream? Would he remember it when he woke up, if he woke up? He felt very weak. His throat hurt and he remembered he had been singing. Why? Once again the dream fled before him as he tried to recapture it.

He felt bereft, without hope. Yesterday—was it yesterday?—he had fought against the voice somehow, but he couldn't remember what he'd done, and anyway it didn't matter. The voice was making it hard to concentrate. Yesterday he had invoked the picture of Solange to aid him, but now he remembered he didn't know where Solange was. Had she gotten to safety when he had called to her? Did the police have her? At least, he thought, she had gotten away from the man in the mask. Or had she? What if there were ten, twenty, a hundred of them, each with his fur and horns and voice like rusty machinery? And what had happened to André, to Patrice? He felt worn out, ground down. He put his fingers in his ears but the voice came through them. There was no way out. He was too weak to stand.

Sleep. Sleep was a way out. He fell into a strange state, half dreaming, his eyes still open to the room's half-light. He sat at a crossroads. It was darker now, almost midnight. The stars had waked overhead but there was no moon. He held something in his hands, something heavy, but for some reason he did not look down to see what it was.

A clock pealed far off. He knew without counting the number of its chimes. He shivered. Someone was coming, someone he had expected. Someone he had dreaded. Everything was still, silent, unmoving. The sound of machinery that he had heard for some reason in the background had stopped. A man stepped out of the darkness.

The man came closer, toward the crossroads. He moved like oil through the dark light. He was the black man, the man of blues legend, not a Negro but a man made out of the darkness itself. The devil.

131

"How did you learn to play so well?" Robert had once asked a blues guitarist in a café on Montparnasse. "Who taught you?"

"Nobody taught me," the guitarist had said. "I sat at a crossroads with my guitar at midnight. It was dark—there wasn't no moon. And a black man came, and he tuned my guitar." The guitarist had paused, as though the story were over. " 'Course," he had said then, "the black man—he took my soul."

Robert trembled. The thing in his hands was, as he had known it would be, a guitar. He held it out to the black man as if to offer it to him, or to ward him off. The black man took the guitar and tuned it. Then he began to play, a sudden dazzling rhythm so quick that Robert could not follow his fingers. The man had guitar picks on his right hand instead of fingernails and instead of the little finger on his left hand he had a bottleneck, the kind of bottleneck blues guitarists used to make their guitars speak in haunting tones. "Come," the black man said. "We will follow the path of stars."

Robert stood, briefly surprised that he was able to. The black man had gone ahead of him, playing a tune that made Robert want to dance and stand still and listen at the same time. He struck stars from his guitar as he played, gold-white stars that hovered about him like fierce animals. "Come," the black man said, turning back to him, and his eyes seemed to be two more stars in his night-black face. As he danced away the stars parted and formed a pathway. Robert followed, unable not to.

How long they traveled this way he never knew. It seemed to him that they left the ground and were traveling in air, gaining altitude, watching the stars pass soundlessly on either side. Once he thought he heard the sound of machinery and he stopped, looking back over his shoulder. "Come," the black man said again. His voice was as deep as seas. "Come, we must not stop."

Robert came on. After a time the night around him seemed to pale. The black man grew sharper in outline, and Robert could see that his clothes, too, were made of night: black coat and trousers, black vest with a gold chain bright as sunrise strung across it. His feet blended with the night-road. The stars began to fade and grow insubstantial, to blend with the lights of the city Robert could see just beyond the black man's shoulder. They were walking toward Rue Fontaine. They had walked backwards through night toward twilight, the most magical hour of Paris.

"We are here," the black man said, his voice seeming to come from the walls and windows and cobblestones of evening. "You are home."

"Is this— Am I really home?" Robert said. "In my own time?"

"Yes," the black man said. His fingers drifted up and down the strings of the guitar. "Good-bye."

"But—" Robert said. "My soul. Does this mean you'll take my soul?" For the first time in his life he wondered if he had one, and what would happen to it if he did.

The black man laughed, a deep, comfortable sound. "Don't believe all you hear," he said. "I must go home now too. Remember me." He went back the way they'd come, leaving a scattering of notes behind him.

Where was he? Robert felt as though he were asleep, still dreaming despite the bright factual lights of the street ahead of him. What if he were still in the room, dreaming that he was home? What if the rest of his life was to be a dream, filled with legends and monsters and twilight? The state where dreams and reality meet, André had said. The true surrealist state. What if the rest of his life were like that? He walked toward the Rue Fontaine, trying to shake off the clothes of unreality he had somehow borrowed.

André was sitting alone in the café. "Robert?" he said. He squinted through darkness to see him. "Is that you? Are you—"

"Hello," Robert said. He sat down heavily. "Yes. I'm back."

"Are you—" André said. "Are you all right?" His eyes never left Robert's.

"I'm all right," Robert said. "Yes, it's really me. I wanted to ask the same about you." He felt closer to his friend than he'd felt in a long time, a kinship, and he laughed. "How—how long have I been gone?"

"A week," André said. "Your concierge said she hadn't seen you."

"I don't suppose she was too worried."

André shrugged. "What—what happened? At the theatre, after the lights went out?"

"I don't know," Robert said. A sudden barb caught at his heart. "Solange. How is she?"

"I don't know," André said. "I managed to get out, and take Patrice—"

"But how?" They stared at each other, two magicians, each assuming the other had pulled off the final grand trick that closed the show. "That light on your cane, and the—the comet?"

"Solange would know," André said. "All I know is that I reached a point where I was able to do it." He spoke slowly, as though talking about someone else. "Time didn't exist. Space didn't either. It must be— It must be that after thinking about surrealism for so long, after living it—"

"Yes," Robert said.

"And finally being among so many people who were living it as well—"

"Yes," Robert said again, hardly daring to breathe. So there was something to it after all, something to surrealism besides all the games and fabulous stories. André the magus.

"And you?" André said. "Where were you? How did you escape?"

Robert told him his adventures. "Ah," André said, moved to wonder at the story of the man with the guitar. "How did he come into it? I wonder. Was he out of your subconscious?"

"Maybe he was," Robert said. He laughed. "If he was, I must really despise my own culture. He comes from a mythology half a world away, from Mississippi, and before that probably from Africa. But what about that—the man in the mask? Who thought him up? What mythology does he come from?"

"He reminds me of the war," André said. "The fanatic dreams of discipline. The mechanized religion of order."

"He reminds me of my concierge," Robert said. "And my family. The way he kept repeating the rules of the status quo." He shuddered. "Only this time I came as close as I've ever come to believing them."

"Everyone who thinks like that had a part in creating him, probably," André said. "All the small minds. The collective desires of the bourgeoisie. Dreams are dangerous things."

Robert shuddered again. "All I know is that I never want to see him again."

They sat for a while, each thinking his own thoughts. Robert, suddenly ravenously hungry, ordered two dinners and began to eat them both. "What about Patrice?" he said between mouthfuls. "You said he was safe?"

"Patrice is here," André said.

"Here?" Robert said, surprised. "How?" And why couldn't I have brought Solange?

"I brought him back with me," André said. "I don't know how. It was the only place I knew to take him. He's out exploring the town with some of the others. They said they'd be back around evening."

"But—how is he going to get back?"

André shrugged. As if on cue the others began coming in, a troupe, an exaggerated comedy show. Louis, Jacques, Antonin, Yves, and yes, there was Patrice in the middle of them, looking intently around him but smiling nonetheless.

"Hello, André." "Robert, you're back!" "He said that Parisian mailboxes didn't exist—" "You should have seen it at night, the strangest spot in all of Paris—" André and Robert had stopped talking as if by prearranged signal. The talk swirled around them. Robert for once felt glad to be among them. He felt very glad to be home.

EIGHT

*"Swarming city, city full of dreams,
where the spectre in broad daylight accosts the
passerby."*
Charles Baudelaire

Robert walked aimlessly through the back streets of Montmartre, the bright wind stinging his ears and drying his throat. Shutters on either side of him remained fastened, mute; lights inside apartments were turned off; flowers in their flowerpots were the only signs of life. Streetlamps hung against the black sky, guiding him from shadow to shadow. Lonely but not desiring company, he turned toward the Rue Fontaine.

A door opened and closed in front of him, spilling out light and music and brightly dressed people. Robert glanced at the sign over the door. Bricktop's. He opened the door and went in.

"Robert!" someone said, a familiar voice. He turned. A woman sitting at one of the tables was waving to him enthusiastically.

"Hélène!" he said, going toward her. "Hello!" She was wearing a long, low-cut dress he had never seen. "What—what have you been up to?"

"Nothing much," she said. "Still working at the old place, the one on Montparnasse. I just came over here for a drink with some of the musicians. But you—how have you been? What have you been doing?"

"Oh, you know," he said. "I've been around." What could he say to her to explain his absence? "I— I got into some trouble a few weeks ago."

"Trouble?" she said, frowning. "What kind of trouble? The police?"

"Sort of," he said, wondering what trouble with the police could mean to her. His father had always spoken for him with the police when he had gotten into trouble.

"Was it something André did?" she said. "One of his crazy ideas?"

"Something like that," he said. "Listen, I don't want to talk about it. Are you working tonight?"

"Tonight's my night off," she said. "I'm just waiting for my friends."

"How would you like to go out with me instead?" he said. "I thought we might celebrate tonight. I sold a novel."

"You did?" she said, distracted as he had known she would be. "But—that's wonderful! Of course I'll go out with you. Just let me talk to the musicians during the break. How do you feel? You must feel great."

"Most of the time," he said. "André threw me out, and then he took me back again."

"Really?" she said. "Why?"

He sighed. Most of André's feuds simply didn't make sense to her. "I'll tell you over drinks," he said.

A few hours later they took the Métro to Montparnasse. Dawn was near; although he had lost a little of his acute sense of direction somewhere in the future, and sometimes saw the newer buildings superimposed over the old ones like a surrealist painting, he had kept his sense of the phases of the night. The air smelled different at dawn.

"That's a nice dress," he said to break the silence. "Is it new?"

"This one?" Hélène said. "Yes, it is. I need all kinds of new clothes now that I've started singing."

"Singing?" Robert said, aware of how inane he must sound. Why was there so much he didn't know about her? "I didn't know—that you sang?"

"Oh, yes," she said, mock-scowling as if to say, It's not much, but it's a job. "Mostly just for myself. But I've sung a few times already at the café. That's where I met all those musicians at Bricktop's. Sometimes they come in to hear me."

"Just to hear you?" he said. "You must be good."

"I don't know," she said. The self-mocking scowl was gone. She was very tired. In the predawn light she looked very beautiful. "They think I am, anyway."

They walked past the cafés of Montparnasse in silence. He was thinking how many independent women he knew in Paris. Bookstore owners, café managers, writers, publishers, and now Hélène, who was going to be a singer. He laughed a little. It was all too much.

"Well, that's great," he said. "That's wonderful."

She looked at him. She had never reproached him

in any way. He had a feeling she didn't care what he did when he wasn't with her, but he owed her an explanation. She was a person, Hélène, not just someone to go to bed with, someone to go to when the conversation at the cafés got too tiresome.

"A strange thing happened to me," he said. He laughed at his lame beginning. Perhaps he shouldn't be a writer. "Well, several strange things, actually." They passed the Dôme. "Let's go in and have a drink, and I'll tell you the rest. All right?"

"All right," she said, smiling. "Take your time."

When they were seated he told her everything, starting with the record at the flea market. He didn't tell her very much about Solange or his love for her, not out of maliciousness or secrecy but because he had a feeling it wouldn't be very polite. Her eyes widened a few times and once or twice she laughed in disbelief, but she didn't interrupt except to ask questions. "So," he said finally. "So that's where I've been."

"It's amazing," she said. "It's like something you'd make up."

"I didn't—" he said, indignantly.

"No, I know you didn't," she said. She put her hand over his. "I said it sounded like it. Like one of those experiments André is always trying. What does he think of all this?"

"Oh, he's delighted," Robert said. "One of his experiments worked."

"And you?" Hélène said. "What do you think?"

"I don't know," he said slowly. "I don't—" He laughed. "I think I've become a revolutionary, but I know for a fact that the revolution won't take place for another forty years. And even then it'll probably fail. So what do I do in the meantime?"

"A revolutionary?" Hélène said, surprised. "You?"

"Me," Robert said. He laughed again. "Solange couldn't do it, and André couldn't do it, but the man in the mask convinced me. If you're not a revolutionary then you're on the side of that. Of the status quo, of the rich getting richer and the poor starving. I'd die before I'd join any side with that—that monster on it."

"And Solange?" Hélène said. "Do you think you'll ever see her again?"

He sighed. He hadn't fooled her—she had seen what was important to him. "No," he said. "I think—I think that's all over. She could be dead. She could have been dead, there in the future." He stopped, briefly confused by syntax. "Anyway, I don't think I'll ever be called back. It failed. Their revolution failed."

"Oh," she said. "What—what do you think you'll do now?"

"I don't know," he said. "It's funny." He wasn't laughing now. "Nothing seems to have changed. After all that, I still go to the cafés every night, still talk to André and the group, still listen to his theories. I even spent a day at the Bureau." He saw her look and said, before she could ask the painful question, "Nothing happened. Nothing happened all day."

"You sold your book," she said. "That's changed."

"That's true," he said. He hadn't thought of that. He warmed toward her, toward Hélène who had become a person and was now even someone to be admired. He had thought he had lost his capacity for surprise. He had thought he had used up all his encounters with the marvelous, as he had used up his inheritance. Perhaps he hadn't. "Where do you want to go now?" he asked. Dawn had broken over the roofs of the city. "Do you want to go to my place?"

"Sure," she said, smiling.

"Whatever happened to your rich American?" he said, paying for their drinks.

"Oh, him," she said. She began laughing and he joined her, though he didn't really see what was so funny. She was a little drunk. "I gave him up." They stepped outside, blinking, two night people lost in the day, and found their way back to the Métro station.

Sometime in the afternoon he awoke screaming, clawing his way out of a nightmare. He had been back in the terrible room again and the man in the mask, his voice sounding like the dull groan of machinery, had begun to move . . . He opened his eyes, feeling himself return to the bed with every nerve in his body. He lay still for a while, watching the sunlight coming in through the window.

Hélène had slept through the nightmare. Perhaps he hadn't screamed after all. He looked at her where she lay next to him in the bed, her mouth slightly open, and he felt a profound sense of depression. That too had not changed. All his attempts to change his life, to transform the world, had come to nothing. He was still going to cafés, still meeting André and the rest of the group, still even sleeping with Hélène. The nightmare was the same as the one that had awakened him all week. Solange was gone. The revolution was gone. All that had been a dream, or it had been reality and this was the nightmare.

He sat up, careful not to wake Hélène. Life goes on, he thought. Things change. The great adventure might be waiting for you even now, right outside your doorstep. The thought did not move him as it once had. I'm getting old, he thought. Doors are closing in every direction. Soon it will be too late. He was not certain what he meant by that.

"Good morning," Hélène said, opening her eyes.

"Good afternoon," Robert said, trying to smile. She has nothing to do with it, he thought. It's not her fault.

They dressed and went outside. He walked with her to the Métro station and she left to go home. He walked back to his apartment slowly, trying to remember when the publisher had said the book was due. He should be home, writing, but he didn't want to be. The day was warm for February.

He went to the Gare du Nord and stood awhile watching the trains come in and leave, the trains that rumbled through so many blues songs like a refrain. Is that what I want? he thought. Should I take a train and go? Right now, for instance, if I take the next train that comes in, I could be on my way to— What time is it? Five-fifteen, on my way to Switzerland. Is that where I want to go? Probably not. The mechanical noise of the trains began to grate on him. He turned and left the station, going toward the Cyrano, where he had been headed all along.

The familiar group sat around the table, talking in low voices. Robert sat next to Yves. "We can't keep him there forever," someone was saying. "And of course he has to eat."

"Who?" Robert said, but no one answered him.

"We could try moving him to the library at the Sorbonne for a few days," someone else said. "Students sleep there all the time."

"And after that?" André said. "We can't keep moving him around like a sack of grain. Sooner or later someone will realize we have Patrice, and then we'll be followed."

"Patrice!" Robert said, louder this time. "What happened to him?"

"The police want him," Yves said.

"The—the police?" Robert said. "What do you mean?"

"What do you think I mean?" Yves said. "André said that the police are after Patrice."

"Have they come in here?" Robert said. "Have you seen them?"

"No," Yves said, more slowly this time. "But once we were walking with Patrice to André's apartment and we heard a strange sort of mechanical sound behind us. André was as frightened as I've ever seen him."

Robert shuddered, a slow shiver that started at his backbone and worked its way outward. "Mechanical," he said, trying to sound casual. He saw from Yves's expression that he hadn't succeeded. "What did it sound like?"

"Like a monotone," Yves said. "You know. Like something played over and over. What is all this about? André just said it was the police."

"No," Robert said. He shuddered again. It followed me back, he thought. It followed me back through the avenues of time. It wants Patrice but it probably wouldn't mind getting me, either. "No, it's not the police."

"What is—" Yves said, but Robert cut him off. "Where is Patrice now?" he said.

"Oh, Patrice," Yves said, laughing a little. "Wait till you hear where we put him. He's in the lighting box at the circus, just down the block. One of my friends is working there till tomorrow." Yves laughed again. "Imagine, a free show every night. I wonder if it'll do him any good. He seemed like such a serious fellow."

Robert hardly heard him. The man in the mask, he thought, feeling cold. The time lines are open—the man in the mask is here.

He hadn't planned to go back to André's apartment with the others after the meeting at the café broke up, but he couldn't walk to his place or the Métro station alone. There was safety in numbers. He found himself walking next to André, shivering from more than the cold.

"The man in the mask followed us back," Robert said.

"Yes," André said. "I didn't believe your description of him but now—" He broke off. "Just hearing him makes me want to run forever, to run until I find a dark hole somewhere to crawl into. . . . All my life my parents, my teachers, everyone has told me I had an overactive imagination, as if that were something shameful to have. But for the first time in my life I would almost give up my imagination, give up everything, just to stop seeing those pictures before my eyes." He stopped and thought awhile. "Do you know," he said finally, "I can almost hear words in that meaningless noise?"

"Those are words," Robert said. "Maybe they're his, maybe they're from some place in your subconscious that you don't want to look into too closely. I don't know. Try not to listen to them."

André stopped. The wind whistled by them loudly, carrying tales. "Did you hear—?" André said.

"No," Robert said, not listening. They hurried, almost running, to catch up with the others.

André's apartment on the Rue Fontaine was bright and welcoming. André's wife Simone had left a fire burning in the fireplace and then gone to bed. Carved masks from Oceania looked down in benediction on the group sitting on secondhand furniture in the living room. Someone went into the kitchen to get drinks.

"Your best childhood memory," Louis said to Yves, sitting next to him.

"The day we went to the beach and I nearly drowned," Yves said. "The bright blue sky, and the green sea, and the blue sky again, over and over like a carousel of blue and green horses that never stopped. That's what I imagined heaven to be like, from that day onward. And then being pulled out of the ocean and made to lie on the warm sand . . . I was almost disappointed." He turned to the student sitting next to him. "Your most erotic memory," he said.

The student laughed a little in embarrassment. No one laughed with him. He looked around the expectant group, opened his mouth, closed it, then said in a rush, "A whore I picked up on the Place Pigalle two days ago." He seemed about to say more but turned to Robert instead and said, "Your most realistic dream."

Robert froze. He looked at André for help, but André was carefully not looking at him. "Oh," he said, trying to sound careless, "I never remember my dreams." André frowned. Robert turned to Louis. "Your favorite method of travel," he said.

The talk at the apartment went on. The firelight washed over the carved masks. Once André reprimanded someone who asked for his neighbor's favorite art piece. "We're not talking about art here," André said. "We're talking about life."

One by one the surrealists went home. It was still dark. "You can sleep on the couch if you like," André said, and Robert was grateful twice over: once for the invitation and once because they hadn't needed to talk about why Robert could not go home in the dark.

"Thank you," he said, settling down on the old couch, knowing from memory where the painful broken springs were. It was almost like the old days when they would sleep at each other's places several times a week.

He turned over to sleep. An insistent hum, like machinery, was already starting to run through his dreams.

He woke around noon, relieved that he hadn't screamed sometime during the night. His dreams had been about trains arriving and departing, about a conductor dressed in black with silver buttons made of stars. The conductor had been driving him somewhere, carrying him away. And behind them the man in the mask came on . . . He turned over, trying to dispel the dream.

"Good morning," André said, coming into the living room and straightening his red tie. "Will you be at the café tonight?"

"Who can plan that far in advance?" Robert said, yawning and sitting up. "Right now I think I'll go home and change. After that, who knows?"

"I thought you'd want to be there," André said. "Because of Patrice."

"Patrice?" Robert said, but he said it softly and André was already gone.

He went to Hélène's café that evening, sitting at a small table near the front to hear her sing. A sense of uneasiness built within him, a sense that something was about to happen or had already happened. A sense that he should be somewhere else.

He did not like the songs Hélène sang, the sentimental old ballads from before the war. But he liked her voice, clear and soaring against the notes of the piano behind her, and he liked the way she carried herself on stage, one light shining upon her as she sang. She went slowly from table to table, pausing a little longer where he sat. He smiled at her. And yet the feeling that he had forgotten something grew—not a dinner date or a friend's birthday but something important, something vital.

At the break he stood and found Hélène. "Let's go," he said, more harshly than he'd intended.

"Go?" Hélène said. "But I still have most of the night—"

"Tell them you're sick," he said. "People must have gotten sick here before." He saw her face and said, "Please."

"But why?" she said. "I can't—I've just started—"

"We have to go," he said. "Someone needs us. Patrice."

"The—the man you told me about?" she said. He nodded. "The one from the future? But how do you know?"

"They're moving him from his hiding place today," he said. "Yves told me yesterday, but I didn't think anything of it. And even this morning, when André asked me if I'd be at the café—I didn't think. I was terrified."

"Of what?" she said.

"Of the man in the mask," he said. She nodded. "I told you about him, but I didn't tell you—I didn't tell you what it was really like. If I had to spend one day with him in that room, just one more day . . . And this time I don't think I'd be able to get out."

"I don't—I don't understand," she said. "What does that have to do with—"

"I don't know," he said. "All I know is—I have a feeling Patrice needs us. He needs us now, before it's too late." He looked at her. He had no right to plead with her this way, he knew. He had never asked anything of her before. He tried to explain. "We need your help, or— I don't know. Maybe not help exactly. I just have a feeling you should be there."

"All—all right," she said, puzzled. "Give me a minute to talk to the manager. And to change." She moved her hand to show her low-cut dress, her high heels, her feather boa.

"No," he said. The urgency was becoming almost physical. "Don't change. We've waited long enough."

"All right," she said, still puzzled. She left him for a while and then came back. "The manager says I can leave now," she said. "He says I even look sick. When will you tell me what this is all about?"

"When I know myself," he said. "Let's go." They took the Métro across Paris to the Cyrano. Robert, running now, hurried inside the café. Hélène followed more slowly on her high heels. André and the rest of the group were not there.

"Come on," he said, running outside. "We'll have to go to the circus now. I hope we're not too late."

"The circus?" she said, breathing hard, hampered by the high heels and the dress. He waited a moment wondering how fast he could run without her, how soon she could catch up if he left her. As he stood on the street corner he heard cries and shouts and turned to see the group coming toward them.

"Hello!" André said, calling to them. "You made it after all."

"Yes," Robert said. "And Patrice—is he—?"

"He's here," André said. The crowd parted a little. "Hello, Robert," Patrice said.

"Is he—are you all right?" Robert said. Patrice nodded. "I ran so fast— I was sure something—" He looked around. "I guess I could have walked," he said. He slumped against a wall, relaxing a little. "I was wrong."

"We still have to move him," André said. "Where are we going tonight?"

"The cemetery," someone said. "One of the vaults."

"The Métro," said someone else. "My cousin's a conductor—we could hide him up front—"

"At the fire station."

"—the police station!"

"At Bricktop's," Hélène said softly.

"The bookstore, in back, where I work . . ."

A soft sound made them turn around. "A car," Yves said, laughing nervously.

The sound grew louder, more insistent—the sound of machinery. "We've got to go," André said. "We've got to decide now and go." He seemed paralyzed by the noise.

"What is it?" someone said.

"This way," Robert said, picking a direction at random. "Let's go."

They followed him. He had no idea where he would lead them, but the need to get away was stronger than any need to stay and plan. The group was slowed by Hélène's heels, by a few people who thought it was all a joke. The night was cold but clear.

"Down here," he said, turning a corner quickly.

"Dead end," Antonin said, calling to him.

"It only looks like a dead end," Robert said, slowing in annoyance. He heard, or thought he heard, the sound of machinery behind them, regular as clockwork. The houses above them leaned together, almost shutting out the stars. "This way." He cut through a courtyard and ducked behind an apartment building.

"I was speaking," Antonin said, hurrying to catch up with him, breathing hard, "metaphorically. A policeman stands at the other end."

Robert nearly stopped. The apartment building had led to another apartment building, and beyond that he could see the street. "Will you for God's sake be quiet for once in your life!" he said angrily, turning the corner into the street. "This is not a game. This is not—" He stopped to catch his breath. Something boomed in the alleyways behind him and he strained to catch the sound. It had sounded like a roof falling. He shuddered, imagining the man in the mask, huge against the stars, knocking the buildings apart in his relentless pursuit. "This isn't one of your stupid surrealist metaphors. This is real, do you understand? Real life. We could die."

"Is there some problem here?" A policeman stepped out of the night, appearing before them suddenly. Hélène, a little distance behind them, was still coming on. She had started to limp. "You'll have to be quiet—people are trying to sleep."

"No," Robert said. "Nothing's wrong." He was quiet, nearly inaudible. All his life he had disliked policemen. "Sorry."

The policeman nodded and let them go. "Not a metaphor at all, then," Louis said.

"Perhaps a metaphor for something else," Antonin said. "Or perhaps not. Perhaps a policeman."

"Definitely a policeman," said Jacques. He opened his hand like a magician. There in the center of his palm, glittering like silver, was the policeman's badge. "Congratulate me, gentlemen. I have never taken one of these before." He closed his fist, opened it again. The badge was gone.

"We've got to get going," Robert said desperately. How had he become the leader of this group of children? How had he become responsible for their lives? He had always been the irresponsible one. "Come on," he said. He led them down another side street.

Yves had stopped. "Look," he said, pointing. A tree grew close to a streetlamp, burning green with lamplight. Beyond the tree the sky was night-black. "I could paint that," he said. "The tree, standing at the gates of dream, and the dream beyond. I know already how I would paint that."

Robert stopped in exasperation. "We've got to go," he said. "Now."

"But where are we?" Yves said. "I want to come back."

"Never mind," Robert said harshly. "I know where we are."

They were walking now, slowing, almost stopping. The mechanical noise had been left behind. Hélène's feather boa slid noiselessly to the ground. "Allow me," Louis said. He picked it up and draped it over his shoulders. Hélène laughed.

"Quiet," Robert said and was immediately sorry he had said it. There was no hurry now, no urgency. They could wander the streets of Paris forever, a party for madmen. Perhaps they would be here forever, a legend, a constellation: the Eternal Travelers. The night stretched out into infinity. He wanted to decide where they would hide Patrice for the night, but his brain would not function. Run! his brain told him. Keep moving! The man in the mask is coming! "André," he said finally. "Where are we going?"

"I don't—" André said. He stopped. "Did you hear that?"

"No," Robert said. The drone of rusty machinery had come up behind them, quite loud now. They began to run, not needing anyone to encourage them, scattering in all directions and then instinctively coming back together for protection. They turned down side streets, alleyways, courtyards, pounded down pavements, ran breathlessly across the main streets, dodging the few cars. Hélène had lost her shoes and was running in her stockings. Robert followed his friends up a steep hill, aware that for once he was in a part of Paris he didn't know. His feet hurt terribly. He wondered if he could carry Hélène.

"Stop," the mechanical voice said behind them. "You cannot outrun me. Wherever you go I will be too. You cannot hide. Stop and we will talk together."

Robert laughed shortly, remembering how they had talked together in the lightless room. A few of the people slowed, hearing the voice. Patrice had turned and was about to say something.

"Come on!" Robert said. "You can't talk to it. Don't be stupid!"

Patrice stopped, confused. He took a few steps toward the voice. The man in the mask came closer and Robert could almost hear him breathing in the darkness, the creature of his nightmare. Ahead of him the group had turned a corner, and suddenly Robert knew where he was. "Come on!" he said to Patrice. "You don't want to talk to him. Believe me!"

Patrice slowly became aware of Robert. He turned away from the man in the mask, his confusion clearing, and he nodded. He and Robert ran around the corner, chasing madly the ones who had gone ahead. Robert hurried toward the head of the group. He knew where they were going now. He would take them to the nearest main street, to bright lights and people, and hope that the nightmare would dissolve into reality. He ran through a corridor between two buildings and across a yard. They turned down another street and then onto the Rue Fontaine, very near to where they had started.

"Robert," the voice said behind him. "You cannot outrun me. I will have you back in the room with me. I will finish what I have started."

"No!" Robert shouted triumphantly, not looking over his shoulder. They were almost there. A few passersby turned to look at him when he shouted, but he paid them no attention. He wondered if they could see the man in the mask, visible now in the street's garish lights, and what they thought. He felt a perverse joy in loosing his nightmare on the streets of Paris.

One block down stood the theatre he and André had gone into that afternoon. It seemed like years ago. Robert turned and pointed to the theatre. A few of them nodded. "What—?" said someone. Can't you see? Robert wanted to say, his energies taken up with running. The man in the mask comes from our nightmares. It won't dare follow us into the Palace of Dreams.

One by one they turned into the theatre. "Wait," the cashier said, seemingly undecided about standing against so many. Robert looked back. Louis had found a fancy woman's hat somewhere to go with the feather boa. The cashier looked wildly at all the people. Don't worry, Robert wanted to say to him. We're all with that man there, the man in the mask. "Robert," he thought he heard the man in the mask say. "Come . . ." Then they were all inside the darkened theatre. He thought he heard the cashier scream.

They crowded in against the wall, unable to find seats in the darkness. On the flickering screen, men with hard faces and beautiful women walked the streets of an American town. Gangsters, Robert thought, wishing he could stay and watch the rest of the movie. His heart pounded heavily, drowning all other sound. His mouth was dry.

A commotion at the doors of the theatre made him turn away. A dark shadow stood at the back of the theatre, motionless as if questing for them. A few of the people inside the theatre had turned back to look at the doors. Someone shouted and was still. Robert felt the taste of fear rush into his mouth. He had made a mistake. The man in the mask had trapped them inside.

Robert looked around hopelessly, seeking an escape. The men and women on the screen had gone into a speakeasy and were drinking and laughing. Beside the screen stood a ladder. Robert felt a strange, exhausted calm come over him. He had found their last chance.

"Come on," he said to the group behind him. "This way." Without letting himself wonder if it would work, he walked to the front of the theatre and moved the ladder against the screen. The screen buckled a little, slightly distorting the men and women in the movie, as the ladder came to rest on the wall behind it.

People in the theatre were moving restlessly. "What the hell do you think you're doing there?" someone shouted to him. "Lights!" someone else called. He began to climb the ladder, slowly, carefully. The surrealists moved down to the front of the theatre, following him. Something hit the screen beside him and he looked back at the audience. The man in the mask had seen him and was coming closer. He turned back to the screen—

The screen was dissolving in front of him like a cloud. He stepped inside, trying to find his footing on the solid floor of the speakeasy. The men and women inside the movie stopped for a moment to look at him. "All right," he said, taking a deep breath. His voice trembled badly, and he wondered how long he would be able to stand. "Everyone—everyone switch drinks."

NINE

"Who speaks of controlling us, making us contribute to the abominable earthly comfort? We want, we shall have the Beyond in our own time. For this we need heed only our own impatience and remain perfectly obedient to the commands of the marvelous."

André Breton

The men and women in the movie were still looking at him when the others began to arrive. André, a wild expression in his usually reserved blue-green eyes. Louis with the feather boa and broad hat. Hélène still shoeless. Patrice looking puzzled. One or two people Robert didn't know, Yves, Antonin, Jacques, a few students.

The dozen or so people crowded into the speakeasy. "Is this—is this part of the movie?" someone asked, whispering. "I mean, are they seeing us now?"

"I don't know," Robert said. The air seemed to flicker in front of him, prisms of light arriving in midair. He put his hands in his pockets to keep them from trembling. This was no dream. In front of witnesses, he had somehow pushed his way inside a movie screen. "Listen," he said.

They paid no attention. One or two were trying to start up conversations with the people in the speakeasy, who were black and white against the bright parrot colors of the surrealists. Someone was ordering a drink. Someone else tried, gallantly, to take a pair of shoes from one of the women for Hélène.

"Listen," Robert said again, louder. "Do you hear anything?"

A few of them paused. "Something . . ." one of them said. Was it the whine of the projector or something else, another mechanical hum? Was it getting louder?

"Come on," Robert said. "We've got to get out of here."

"Wait a minute," Jacques said. "I've been talking to this fellow here, over by the bar. He says he's starting to build an empire, might have a job for me in Chicago—"

"Are you crazy?" Robert said. "None of these people are saying anything. Films are silent, for God's sake."

"Yes, well, why don't you just go along without me?" Jacques said. "I'll see you somewhere later."

Robert nearly laughed. Maybe this was the way out. Maybe the man in the mask, confronted with twelve lunatics, would just turn around and go home. Robert wanted to stay as badly as anyone. What a chance, he thought. What possibilities.

The mechanical noise grew louder. "Listen," Robert said to Jacques. "You could die if you stayed here. It's your choice. Do you want to get out and survive till 1929, or do you want to take four years off your life? It doesn't really matter to me."

"What's wrong with you, Robert?" Jacques said. "You used to be able to take things easier."

"I've seen something," Robert said. "Something you'd better pray you'll never ever see in your short blissful foolish life. After this is over I'll take things as easy as you like. Easier. Now come on."

"This way!" André said, calling to them. "There's a door over here that leads outside."

A few of the group were beginning to follow André outside. The characters in the movie turned back to each other, returning to the thread of the plot. I suppose, Robert thought, we weren't really real to them either.

"The chance of my life," Jacques said mournfully. "The one chance of my life, good-bye forever."

Now what, Robert thought, stepping after him. Another movie set? The streets of Chicago? Back to Paris?

Clear white light hit him. A broad white street stretched off into the distance. White slabs and pillars ran along the road. "Dear God," someone said. "Where are we now?"

A long shadow of a man appeared at the side of one of the far pillars. The man stepped around the pillar, followed by five or six more people. Robert and his small group stood still under the heavy bright light, their carnival colors bleached in the sunshine. Robert felt small, insignificant. They stood silent, waiting.

"Hello," one of the people said. "We're glad to see you could make it."

"Make it where?" Robert said. "Where are we?"

"Back," the man said. "You're back in the future."

"The future—"

"Where—"

"—rocket ships—"

"—don't understand—"

The future. Robert searched the group for Solange, searched foolishly, since he had already seen that she wasn't there. "The—the future," he said. "It's changed quite a bit since I was here last."

The man laughed. He was older than the others, with white hair and a tanned, lined face. "We're even further into the future than that," he said. "As far from 1968 as you were, but in the other direction."

"Oh," Robert said. There were a million questions he wanted to ask, but there was only one real question. Solange. Where was she? His heart shook with the possibility that he might see her again.

"Well," the man said, seeing Robert's indecision. "We can sit down somewhere and get comfortable, if you'd like that. This street wasn't built for comfort." There seemed to be more to his words than the surface meaning. "My name's Henri, by the way."

"Robert," he said. Henri nodded, as if he had known. Robert turned back to his group. "Come on, people," he said. They had been talking among themselves, looking around in wonder. Nothing kept them silent for very long. A few had already started to drift away. "Henri's going to take us someplace else." He turned to go with Henri, without checking to see if they were following him. He felt like a pilgrim, a traveler beginning a long journey but with the destination known. Hope had taken root in his heart once again. They set off down the white road.

Behind him he heard, or imagined he heard, the sound of gears shifting.

Lisa Goldstein

The road was extraordinarily hot. They were caught
between the fierce white light of the sun and the blank
glare of the road itself. Robert took his coat off and
dropped it to the road. A few of the others, he saw,
were doing the same. An uneasiness, almost a feeling of
dread, came over him. Where was Henri taking them?
He had seemed friendly enough, but who was he?
Whose side was he on? The road, the concrete slabs,
the pillars seemed to go on forever. Robert slowed.
What if it was a trap?

The sun winked out suddenly. The road and the
pillars stood forth in astonishing whiteness. Before he
could blink, the sun shone down on them again, as hot
as before. He looked around carefully. What had happened? Had he imagined it? One or two others were
slowing, uncertain. The heavy heat made it difficult to
talk.

"What—?" Robert said. Henri did not seem to
hear him.

"Who are you, anyway?" André said, louder. "Where
are we going?"

The pillars, the road, the slabs turned night-black.
This time the sun stayed as it was. Robert slowed,
feeling almost blinded. The road and the slabs turned
white again, silent, dull, endless. "All right," Robert
said. It was an effort to talk. "Where the hell are we?"

"Around the corner," Henri said. Robert saw with
surprise that Henri was having difficulty speaking too.
"Almost there."

The road curved almost imperceptibly. Robert would
never have noticed the curve if Henri hadn't mentioned
the corner. It seemed to take forever to round the
curve. The road changed slowly. Trees, unbearably green
against the white landscape, stood along the side now
instead of pillars. The road turned slowly from white to

160

gray to earth-brown. The trees grew closer, more numerous. The shade dappled the sunlight. Robert felt as though he had carried a heavy burden for many miles and was now finally allowed to set it down. He began to walk faster.

Grass grew on the road. He saw Hélène run her feet through the cool grass, pleasure on her face. "Where are we?" Robert said. "This isn't Paris."

"The outskirts," Henri said. He sat down heavily, and the rest of them sat in a semicircle facing him. "That's the road the army takes. We had to change it because of the war."

"War?" Robert said. He looked around. "Is what happened on the road—was that because of the war?"

"What happened?" Henri repeated thoughtfully. "That's hard to say. I don't know what you saw. Different people see different things."

"I don't—I don't understand," Robert said.

"It's always difficult to walk down that road," Henri said. "We created it to be a negative place, a place as unwelcome as possible. For the rest—well, your subconscious takes over."

André looked up, fascinated.

"We fight with the only tools we have," Henri said. "The tools given to us by the surrealists long ago. Art, magic, dreams."

André started to say something. Robert never heard him. Past the trees, across a small field, Solange was walking toward them. With a feeling of inevitability, of déjà vu, Robert stood up and ran to her. They met in the middle of the field, laughing.

"Are you something from my subconscious too?" Robert said. "Something from my desires this time, instead of my nightmares?"

"No," she said. "Here I am. I had to come."

He put his arms around her, delighting in the solid feel of her. She was here at last, his at last. They had pursued each other through the conflicting currents of time only to meet here in this place, free of the past and the future, here in the present moment. It was time, and more than time. He kissed her. "I love you," he said softly.

They drew apart slowly. He kept his arms around her, his heart pounding at his boldness. "Come on," she said, almost whispering. Her eyes were dark, unreadable. "I'm sharing a place with some other people."

She led him across the field. Had that house always stood there, or had it just now materialized before them, another object of his dreams? It seemed large, many-storied, a hedge around it and a lake behind it where a few people were rowing. They went inside—it was unlocked—and passed through a corridor with doors on either side. Once he thought he saw something through an open doorway that looked like a hall of mirrors. She went up a flight of stairs and opened a door.

Once inside he had to stop and catch his breath. A strange feeling of wonder suffused him. This was her room. All objects were at once holy and profane: he had known that, it seemed, all his life, despite his fairly strict Catholic upbringing. Yet here in her room he felt it more clearly than he had ever before. This was the table she sat at, to write, to eat, to read. This was her chair. That was her bed.

She took his hand and led him to the bed. "I wanted to explain something to you," she said, sitting close to him. He nodded. Her nearness made it difficult to concentrate. "It seems—" She stopped, at a loss. She laughed a little and went on. "We fight the revolution, in part, for love," she said. "So that people will be free to love, free to follow their desires. Not trapped into thinking that love is just another commodity, like laundry soap."

He opened his mouth to say something but she stopped him. "No, let me finish," she said in her clear voice. "I know this sounds like a speech—I'm sorry. I've been thinking about this for a long time. You see," she said, looking away from him, unable to meet his eyes, "I knew all that. But I was so caught up in the strike—so busy fighting—I wanted to put love away until another time, until I had time to think about it. But I was wrong. Do you understand what I'm saying?"

"Yes," he said.

"And then— Well, I thought of you as a person in history. I'd been reading about you for so long, reading and dreaming . . . When I— When I started to walk through time, when we started to think about contacting you—suddenly my life wasn't real any more. Whoever I was seeing wasn't real to me. When I was seeing Paul, for example. Only you were real, and you weren't even there. You were a dream." He was nodding, amazed at her understanding, at how well she had spoken his feelings. He could not trust himself to answer her.

"I dreamed you would love me," she said, looking at him boldly now as if reading his thoughts. Her face was flushed. "But I couldn't believe it when you actually did, couldn't believe my luck. I didn't want to go any further. I was afraid you'd vanish, afraid I'd made you up. I was afraid I'd wake up."

"No," he said. "No. I love you."

She held him for a long time. "It's ridiculous," she said finally, pulling away from him a little. "We don't even live in the same time."

"I don't care," he said. "That's not important."

"You're right," she said. "You were the true revolutionary. Despite your denials. You were the one following your desires. I was trying to ignore mine. Hoping they'd go away and come back when I was ready for them."

"Quiet," he said. He leaned over and kissed her. Desire rose strongly within him. "True revolutionaries don't talk so much."

She laughed. She kissed him back with fire, with passion. It was worth everything, worth waiting for, he thought. He began to undress her, marveling, her body opening like a rose before him.

Afterwards they lay together side by side, one nestled within the other. Their legs were bent; their hands were clasped together; they seemed to be running. He dreamed that they *were* running, she leading him, going toward something far ahead in the distance. There were bright colors, laughter, snatches of good music. He saw some people wearing masks, not the distorted metal and fur mask that he feared but bright open masks, masks that revealed more than they concealed. A black man played guitar. And behind them, in the darkness, something was following.

He awoke. He hadn't screamed. Lying there beside her, he had the feeling that they had made it to safety. He turned over and smiled to himself. She was still asleep.

After a while he got up and walked around the small room. He touched the chair, the table, the plants she had growing in the window. He opened the door; it led to the corridor and to other people's rooms, but he wasn't interested in them. He closed the door again.

In the corner was something that looked like a record player. He went over and knelt beside it. It looked horribly complex, with buttons and knobs he had never seen before, but everything was labeled and within minutes he was hunting through the stack of records beside it. He found the record he wanted, as he knew he would. "The Moon's Bright Falling Towers."

She awoke when she heard the music and smiled at him. It was strange to see the contrast between the two—the vibrant alive singer on the record and the woman just waking up in bed. And yet they were unarguably the same person. Some of the instruments on the record were unknown to him and some of the rhythms were hard to follow, but the music had the same intensity, the same truths as the blues recordings he had listened to in his cold apartment. The record was as important to him as he had known it would be. He would listen to it a hundred times.

Some of his contentment ebbed away as they dressed together. We don't even live in the same time, she had said. It was impossible, ridiculous. That wasn't important, he had said. But it was. The currents of time had thrown them together for a while and might just as easily tear them apart. Who knew when they would meet again? It's not fair, he thought. I've known love for the first time, and now I'm going to be denied it. He felt angry at someone, angry and ill at ease.

They went outside, walking slowly back to the road. André and Henri were sitting where they had left them, deep in conversation. André looked up and nodded to them as they came nearer. "Look," he said. He held out his hands, palms up. A flower grew from one of them, leaves unfolding as it did so. He clapped his hands and the flower disappeared.

Robert blinked. "How—?" he said.

"It's magic," André said, as if that were an explanation. "I've known ever since I was a child that magic existed somewhere, that there was a realm, if only we could get to it . . ."

"We've freed the subconscious," Henri said. "We want to live in a world without limits."

Robert nodded, sitting down beside them. Solange sat next to him. He held his hand out as he had seen André do. Grow, he thought. Grow, dammit. Nothing happened. He shrugged.

"And you were the one who brought me here," André said to Robert. "I have to thank you for that, and I don't know if I ever can."

"Don't thank him yet," Henri said. "You may not like it here. The war is coming to a close, for good or bad."

"What war?" Robert said. He looked around uneasily. He wondered if he would ever escape war, the trenches and the barricades and that strange awful road. "I haven't seen any fighting. It all seems so peaceful to me."

"Paris is on strike," Henri said. "Paris, and parts of France. And other parts of the world, too, though it's hard to get news here. The governments are worried, of course. They've banded together, some of them. They think that if they can crush us, crush Paris, everyone else will be demoralized. But this time," Henri smiled harshly, almost grimacing, "this time I think we're going to make it." The lines on his face were dark against his skin.

"You should see it, Robert," Solange said. "The joy in the streets, like in sixty-eight. Only this time it's real, it's not some fad. The people realize they've been lied to once too often. Things were getting tight, very rough, before the strike."

He smiled at her. "I'd like to see it," he said. He realized that he meant it, that he had truly and finally become a revolutionary. There was too little joy in the world where he came from. "But what's all this about—about magic? The subconscious?"

"We realized that we couldn't fight with their weapons," Henri said. "Or that we could, but that in the end we would be no better than they were. The avenues of time had broken down—reality is pretty distorted—and we contacted Solange and her group. Or they contacted us, I'm not sure which. Together we learned a few things about reality. We built the road—which may or may not be real, I don't know—and we helped you get here. Solange even went back once to get that damned stereo."

"Hey," Solange said, her eyes flashing. "I need that stereo."

Robert took her hand. "So do I," he said.

Patrice ran up to them across the field. "They've come!" he said, breathing hard. "We saw some people marching down the road. I think the army is here."

"Watch," Henri said to them. Robert had started to get up. "We'll show you how we fight them."

The rest of the surrealists had come up after Patrice. Someone had given Hélène new clothes, Robert noticed—pants and comfortable-looking shoes. Henri's group, the people they had met on the road, stood behind the trees and watched the road. Each one carried an unfamiliar-looking instrument.

The soldiers began to straggle up the road. Some looked around, clearly uncertain. Others came doggedly along the path, not looking up. The leader walked slowly, as though cutting his way through a jungle. The group by the side of the road took out their instruments and began to play.

The music was wavering, unstructured. It raised questions that weren't answered, started tunes but didn't finish them. The soldiers slowed. A few of them stopped, puzzled. Two or three groups began talking in low tones.

One or two of the soldiers turned to go back. Someone began to argue, his voice loud against the soft music. More and more of the soldiers were going back the way they had come. The leader straightened slowly and marched to the front of the line to lead the retreat.

"No, no!" someone said, shouting, but his voice was drowned by the band, which had started to play a loud military march. The soldiers went back down the road in triumph.

Robert laughed until tears came to his eyes. "It's beautiful!" he said. "If only— If only—" He was laughing too hard to complete the sentence.

André, who almost never laughed, was smiling. Solange had borrowed one of the instruments and was trying to play it. "That was easy," Patrice said. "Almost too easy."

"And unfortunately that was only an advance, a scouting party," Henri said. "The rest of the army will be here soon, and we won't be able to pull that trick on all of them at once. The best thing would be to leave some people here and go on to Paris. What do you think?"

The people carrying the instruments nodded. "How are we getting to Paris?" Robert asked.

"How?" Henri said. "We'll take the Métro, of course."

The Métro, surprisingly, had not changed very much. The design of the cars and the seats inside were different but Robert recognized most of the lines and even knew in which direction they were traveling. "Oh, but it's very different," Henri said when Robert said something to him. He smiled. His eyes were youthful against the lines of his face. "The workers control it now." They got out near the Sorbonne.

Though the Métro hadn't changed, Paris, when they got outside, was astonishingly different. An archaeologist might have been able to reconstruct his home, his time, from fragments, from window designs and door frames, but Robert was lost. And over everything lay a feeling of unreality, a sense that the city might lift itself like a wave or shatter into a thousand pieces. A building of twenty stories seemed to move as Robert watched it and once he thought he saw Sacre Coeur where Notre Dame should have been. The Eiffel Tower seemed to undergo a hundred transformations in an eye-blink: it became rectangular, rounded, stretched itself out and buckled like a roller coaster. Robert had once seen a book showing all the plans submitted for the design of the Eiffel Tower. It seemed now that the Tower was trying to recapture all of them in the space of a second. The past had melted, was fluid. All present moments were possible.

André had moved closer to him. He looked lost but exhilarated. The wild expression had returned to his eyes. "Where—?" he said.

"Don't count on me for this one," Robert said. "I'm lost too."

It seemed to him that they had stood there for only a few minutes when someone shouted, "Look! The helicopters!"

Robert looked up. Above him loud airplanes—no, they weren't airplanes—the helicopters clacked mechanically in circles. He fought an instinct to duck. "They've decided not to take the road then," Henri said.

"I wonder if they got through our defenses on the Seine," someone said anxiously.

"We'd better get going," Henri said. "We don't have much time."

He could never remember, later, all the events of the next few hours. He was never even sure if it had been hours, or minutes, or days. Perhaps he had spent months fighting a phantom enemy, an enemy that would swoop overhead and spray them with the clatter of machine-gun bullets and leave as quickly as they had come.

There were troops on the ground, too, and it was these troops that he was left to deal with as best he could. He never knew who it was who caused the distortions of reality, the strange waves that would break over them and leave them disoriented, whether it was Henri, André or one of the others fighting with them. He wondered as he fought if he could be the one responsible.

The wave came and a maze of mirrors appeared between him and the group of soldiers in front of him. The soldiers broke through the maze with their rifles, smashing the mirrors with the butts. The mirrors reflected back the grinning advancing troops, stretching their bodies to thinness, compressing them to squat unrecognizable shapes. One soldier looked into a mirror and ran away screaming. His reflection remained in the mirror, a snarling mask of fur and horns and steel.

The next minute some of the surrealists were wearing masks too. André's was bright silver, unsmiling, with sharp planes and cheekbones. Antonin had sharp ivory tusks and fur. Solange was a dragon. One of the soldiers threw up his rifle and shot wildly. The shot echoed down the wide street.

The soldiers came on, more and more of them. The surrealists threw up a forest of trees, an underwater grotto, a shower of stars. The streets shifted beneath them: one soldier shouted in surprise as he ran around a corner and ended up back among his own men.

André stood out in front of everyone, his hair blowing around his face. His eyes shone wildly. A soldier ran up toward him, holding his rifle close. The rifle became a fish and the soldier stopped quickly, dropping it with a look of disgust.

Antonin screamed. "My head!" he said. His boar's mask lay on the ground next to him. "My head my head my head!" He clapped his hands to his ears, bending back in agony. Fireworks pounded the sky. Antonin sat on the ground, holding his head between his knees. He seemed to be crying.

He really is crazy, Robert thought, seeing him as if for the first time. He felt a small tendril of pity for him. André's going to throw him out soon, he thought, seeing Antonin's future with bright clarity. He'll be the next one excommunicated. Crazy people have their own ideology.

A shot exploded close to him and he jumped. What a time to think about the future, he thought. As if we could know if we'll have a future to go back to. A large brightly-colored bird swooped low over the man who had shot at him and gripped the man's rifle in its talons. The man screamed and held on.

"Close one," Louis said, appearing next to him.

Robert turned to look at him. "Yes," he said.

The fighting seemed to have stopped for the moment. Antonin had created a huge steel wall and was struggling to hold it in place between him and the soldiers. "I can't—I don't really know what I'm supposed to be doing here," Louis said. He laughed a little. "I feel a little out of place."

"I don't know what I'm supposed to be doing either," Robert said. "I guess we just do the best we can."

"Yes, but—" Louis said. "But it's all so—so unstructured. In the army at least you knew what to do. I hated the army, but at least you knew what to do."

With the same prophetic clarity that had enabled him to see Antonin's future Robert saw Louis after they returned home. Louis would join some sort of ideology— left or right, it didn't matter. Louis would look for structure, for guidelines. He had seen imagination set free and it scared him. "Well," Robert said, saddened by this vision of his old friend, "we should probably get back. I don't know how much longer Antonin can hold out."

A helicopter clattered by overhead, firing machineguns, and they ducked. The large bird flew after it, squawking when it realized it couldn't reach it. The steel wall buckled and came down. A forest of glass grew up around them, shattering with beautiful sounds when hit.

Solange was running, dodging soldiers, cars, cobblestone barricades. Three or four soldiers ran after her but she outdistanced them. They slowed several times but she was never in one place long enough for them to take aim at her. Suddenly she turned around. She seemed to blend with the mask she wore, to grow claws and scales and become a dragon. A claw scratched the ground and flames shot up, dividing her from the soldiers. Sparks fell to the ground: each spark took root and became a rosebush with flame-red roses. The bushes grew together and formed a thorny wall. Robert, watching her, smiled suddenly. She was undefeatable.

A moment later she came up to him. She had taken off her dragon mask and was shaking her dark hair free. "Good work," he said, kissing her.

"Thank you," she said. "I know."

Hélène was laughing. A bit tentatively she pointed at a spot farther down the street, in front of an oncoming tank. A piano grew up out of the road just in time for the tank to collide with it. Cursing, uniformed men got out of the tank and heaved the piano off the road. Hélène laughed again. As the tank started up again she created a harp, a tuba, a set of drums. Unlike everyone else, Hélène knew exactly which of the creations were hers. She didn't care what anyone else did, but she knew she would never kill anyone. A large chandelier fell from the sky and landed in front of the tank.

Someone pulled at Robert's sleeve and he turned around. It was Jacques. "This is paradise!" he said. "I can barely believe it. My collection is immeasurably richer. Look at this!" He held out his hand. Robert saw military insignia he didn't recognize, buttons with hard, dull surfaces, coins with unimaginable dates.

Jacques closed his palm and opened it again. The things were gone. "Things like that keep happening," he said, sounding surprised. He closed and opened his palm once more. The small collection reappeared. "It's so hard— It's hard to hold on to anything any more. I think André's right. I used to be pretty good with sleight of hand, but I think here— I think magic really works." He looked almost frightened.

"And what are you doing?" Robert said, suddenly angry. "You're collecting trash. Why aren't you out there fighting with the rest of us?"

Jacques looked at him with vague surprise. "I didn't ask to come here," he said. "I didn't ask to fight this war. All I ask is to die at my own time and my own place."

Robert blinked. That was certainly true. No one had asked Jacques if he had wanted to come along.

"Well, get out of our way then," he said, irritated. "Go somewhere else to find your junk. This is dangerous." As if to punctuate his words a shot exploded overhead. Someone screamed.

"All right, I will, but first I want—I want to show you—" Jacques said, tugging at his sleeve once more.

"Jacques," Solange said, interrupting. "Do you know you've been written up in the history books?" Jacques fell back a pace. His mouth worked but he made no sound. "Do you want to know if you live or die? If you attempt suicide, and if it's successful?"

Jacques took another step back. "I— No, I—" he said. He turned and fled.

Robert laughed for a long time. "I didn't know—" he said, trying to speak. "I didn't know you could be so cruel," he said finally. He wiped his eyes. "My God, that was cruel."

Solange laughed. "Do you want to know?" she said teasingly. "It could prove useful some day."

Robert shook his head. For the third time that day he saw into the future, saw with some surprise and not a little sadness that Jacques would indeed kill himself on the date he chose. He shook his head again, this time to clear it. For a moment he felt bereft. The world would be a less colorful place with Jacques gone.

The street washed out, became unsolid. A moment later reality returned like the tide going out. Robert took a step, stumbled, sought solid footing. Yves stood to the side, smiling absently as the street ran before him like water. "What a place," he said. "To paint with the world as a canvas. How clever of you to bring us here, Robert." He had forgotten that they were fighting a war, perhaps had never known. For Yves, the painter of dreams, this was a dream escaped somehow into the real world.

174

And André still stood in front, the director at the Theatre of Dreams. What would happen to André after the war they fought was over? The prophetic sight that had come over Robert three times so far refused to come again. Would André return to the past? Would he survive, would he continue on from adventure to adventure? Once again his friend was a mystery to him.

The streets became darker. For a moment the sun seemed to grow smaller instead of setting. Then night, the night of the outside world, came to the streets of Paris. The gunfire slowed and finally stopped. The houses grew dark and solid around them.

Someone built a bonfire. By its red, wavering light Robert could see the barricades of cobblestones and overturned cars and uprooted trees, the reality he had missed while fighting the war of the fantastic. He laughed wearily. Some things would never change.

They drew around the bonfire for warmth. Henri was talking to Solange, and Robert sat down beside them. Henri's dry voice and the fire's crackle were the only sounds. After the battle it seemed unnaturally quiet.

"I was about your age in sixty-eight," Henri said. "Maybe a little younger." He laughed. "Just think, you might be alive today," he said. "Maybe you'll even meet yourself."

Solange laughed. Robert saw her shudder and he put his arm around her. "I'd rather not," she said.

"Anyway, I was about your age," Henri said. "I was a good student—I wasn't like you, thinking and talking about revolution. I went to classes, went to parties, you know what student life is like." He spoke quietly, naturally. His life was as clear and open as a map, without shading.

"And then everyone went on strike. And suddenly

everyone was saying, 'Power to the imagination,' and, 'Live without dead time'—you know, all the slogans that have become so famous. And for the first time—you'll find this hard to believe, but it was really the first time, the first time in my life—I realized that life could be lived another way. That it didn't have to be lived the way my friends and I were living it. The realization—well, it was like being knocked down suddenly and without warning. I was euphoric for months. Even after the revolution failed. Because there was something else to life, you see, something besides what I had been taught."

Solange smiled. The firelight washed over her face. "And then you lived to see it happen again," she said.

"But all that almost doesn't matter," Henri said, talking with great animation. "All it means is that everyone suddenly started to agree with me."

Solange laughed. One by one, people were dropping off around the fire. Robert saw Jacques come in from the surrounding night and huddle by the fire to keep warm. He lay down next to Solange and slept. Solange's voice and her laugh cut through his sleep but there were no dreams.

The defectors began coming in before sunrise. Robert woke and lay silent for a while, listening to one of them talk to Henri.

"There was this statue," the soldier was saying. "I don't know who he was, some old guy from before I was born. And the next time I passed it there was some kind of—one of those things made out of all different colored parts—a mobile. And the statue was gone. Well I remember thinking that that was a lot of work to go to, and in the middle of a war, too. And then the next time I passed it the old man was back, but he had thrown back his head, and he was—he was laughing.

"I don't know," the soldier said. "I mean, you may not believe me. I'm from the country, and that's where I've been for most of the war. But from what I hear there are things here that are a lot stranger than what I've seen. So what I want to know is, what—well, what's going on? Are you people magicians?"

Henri looked at him gravely. "No," he said. "No, or if we are then everyone else is one too. We're living without limits, that's all. We don't believe everything we've been taught."

The soldier looked confused. "I don't understand," he said. "I don't believe everything I've been taught either, but I couldn't move a statue."

"Stay with us," Henri said. "Watch us. You'll understand."

"Can I?" the soldier asked. "I don't know if I go along with everything you believe in, but I've seen things on the other side—well, I know I can't fight for them. And you people seem to be having a better time."

Henri smiled broadly. "You'll do," he said. "Put down your gun. I think we're about to get breakfast soon."

Breakfast? Robert thought, becoming aware of how hungry he was. He sat up. Some men and women carrying wicker baskets had come up to the dying fire. "It's becoming harder and harder to slip by the army," one of the women was saying in a broad country accent. "They're trying to close down the Métro now, but I don't think they can. Of course some stations are safer than others, but everyone knows that. I think this is their last attempt before they give up." She opened the basket and began taking out eggs, bread, butter, glass jars of milk.

"Good morning, Robert," Henri said, seeing him

stand and stretch. "I thought the food would rouse you. Would you like some breakfast?"

"Of course," Robert said, grinning. "Thank you."

"Eat well," Henri said. "We have a long day ahead of us. But I think—" he said, squinting into the sun coming up in the east—"I think this will be the last day." He tore off a slice of bread and began to eat.

The shots started up again during breakfast. Eggs and bread were hastily dropped as people ran for safety behind the barricades. A flock of swans, at first tentatively sketched in and almost transparent, rose from the barricades to meet the machine-gun fire. The swans grew more solid. The battle had started.

An hour later Robert was busy creating a railroad line. He wanted to see the soldiers step on board the train, which would at first seem straight enough, and then be carried back to their starting point. The shots had slowed down and Robert could hear as much as five minutes of silence before they started up again. He wondered if the army had been weakened by deserters.

The train refused to come clear. Once he had the cars but the track wavered and finally disappeared. Once he had everything but the engine and then lost it all by concentrating on that. A strange, unhealthy silence had descended over the streets, as though everything had stopped at once. Robert looked up. Illusions were wavering, the wind blowing them like paper. He looked for his train but it had disappeared.

He was the first to hear the mechanical drone coming from one of the side streets. His first impulse was to run, to leave everyone he cared about and try to make it back to his time and the brightly lit cafés on the Rue Fontaine. He wanted to hide, to curl up behind one of the overturned cars and hope that he would be overlooked. He stood where he was, fighting the panic.

"I don't think it's real," Henri was saying to one of the defectors. "I think it's a shape we make up, the way we perceive the enemy. They're using our fears against us, that's all." He did not sound as though he believed it.

"I had a dream once—a nightmare—" the defector said. He seemed about to run.

The man in the mask came closer. He was larger than Robert remembered, his shoulders seeming to dwarf the houses, the cars. His mask filled the sky, blotting out the sun in some malign eclipse. "Drop your weapons," he said without inflection. "Stop your childish games. Come back to work. You've been on vacation too long. There's nothing wrong with work. Work is good for you. Work builds character."

"We want to work for ourselves!" Henri said. "Not for others."

The man in the mask ignored him. Perhaps he hadn't heard anything. "Don't you think it's a shame the way you've neglected your work?" he said. "Civilization needs order. Civilization can't function while you're away, while you're on vacation. Come back to work."

"We don't need your civilization," Henri said, but this time only Robert heard him.

If I could just build that train, Robert thought. The train, or a wall, or something . . . Nothing happened. He could not remember how he had created illusions, or even if it had been he creating them and not someone else. His mind was frozen with fear.

The soldier next to Henri moved suddenly, raising his gun up at the man in the mask. A shot rang out over the street. The man in the mask laughed, a sound like gears grinding. "Don't you think you can hurt me," he said. "I'll remember you." The soldier threw down his gun and ran down the street. The sound of his feet hitting the pavement echoed off the walls of the houses and went on for a long time.

I've got to do something, Robert thought. I've got to . . . Henri had gone very pale. It's not often someone sees the ruin of his dreams twice in his lifetime, Robert thought, moved by pity. I've got to—I've got to remember something—

Remember me, someone said, behind him.

Robert jerked around. They were all standing as he had been, watching the man in the mask with horror and fascination. A few of them looked at Robert, puzzled. No one had spoken.

Remember me, the voice said again, coming from another direction. Who—? Robert thought.

He stood in a street in Paris in daylight, but lying over that like transparent film was a crossroads at midnight. There was nothing for miles but the flat dead land, no wind, no noise but the crickets and once in a while the lonesome approaching sound of a car on a solitary errand. A few silver guitar notes danced out into the quiet of the night.

"Help—" Robert said, hardly aware that he was speaking. "Help me—"

The black man was walking lightly to the crossroads. His gold watch chain dazzled like the sun. It's impossible, Robert thought. How can something I made up help us stand against—against that? The man played a few high notes, an invitation. More people believe with me this time around, Robert thought, feeling hope return. Enough time has passed for them to learn the lessons of surrealism. This time we might make it.

"I told you," the black man said in his deep voice. The Paris street materialized around them again. "I told you to remember me."

His fingers fell with hammered precision on the strings of his guitar. The bottleneck slid up and down the strings until the guitar seemed to be crying. The rhythms grew faster, more complex.

Other instruments joined in—a harmonica, a bass, a piano. Robert could not tell where they were coming from. The music grew louder, louder and faster, faster, until the black man's hands seemed a blur, seemed to divide and become three, four hands, all playing the same guitar. Now one was hitting the body of the guitar to count the rhythm and one was picking the strings and one was chording and one ran the bottleneck up and down the strings, up and down, creating that eerie sound, a crying sound . . .

And through it all the black man grinned wider and wider, the grin of a man possessed by the devil or of the devil himself. Light flashed off his big gold tooth, off the guitar which he twirled over his head or behind his back without missing a beat. He danced, he kicked his heels, he did somersaults, weaving an arc of light around him as he moved.

The music seemed to come from everywhere. Everything was dancing, the houses, the trees, the streetlamps, the street itself. The men and women behind the barricades began to unfreeze, to move in time to the music. Some of them were humming.

A clatter of bullets drowned them out. A few of the people who had ventured out in front of the barricades were hit. One or two were screaming. "Come back!" Henri called, standing and looking out over the barricades. "It's not over! Get back behind—" A bullet hit him in the chest and he fell, a trickle of blood running from his mouth.

Robert looked at him in horror. He crouched low behind the barricades. The music, incredibly, had not stopped. Now the guitarist was weaving the sounds of the bullets and the drone of the man in the mask into his music. Robert peered over the barricades to watch him. Nearly all the machine-gun fire was directed at the black man now but none of it was hitting him.

"Go home," Robert said softly, almost to himself. The memory of Henri, a red stain seeping through his shirt, made him angry, and the anger and hatred were enough to push him forward. "Go home." The man in the mask turned to him, leering, and he felt a fear greater than he had ever known in his life. Henri kept him steady.

"Go back to my nightmares, back to where you came from!" he said, standing up and shouting out over the barricades. He was almost singing. The music filled him, sang inside of him, turned him to music. "We don't need you here."

Antonin looked at Robert with admiration. "When did you become a magus?" he said, amazed. "You were dead, but now—"

The man in the mask headed toward Robert, distracted. The black man came closer to him, dancing a circle around him. The man in the mask grew smaller. His mechanical voice fell into the wild rhythms of the black man's guitar, or the black man played counterpoint to the droning sound until he had melded it with his music. "Go back," the man in the mask said like a broken record. "Go back. To work. Go back."

The black man was dancing around him, drawing out complex strands of rhythm. The music seemed to hold him. The man in the mask shrank back further and further within the web of music, growing smaller and smaller. For an instant he seemed to become a small man with round glasses and a bowler hat. Then he disappeared.

The shooting stopped. The soldiers put down their guns and ran. A great sigh of exultation came up from the city. Car horns honked. Fireworks were set off.

Solange came over to Robert and put her arms around him. "We made it," she said. "We won."

"Yes, but—" he said. "But Henri—" He knelt down to where Henri lay. Henri's breathing had stopped. "He never made it," Robert said. "And he worked so hard." He stood up, feeling angry and somehow cheated. His hand felt for Solange's.

A great ring of fire appeared before them. "You can stay here, and be returned to the past," the black man sang. "Or you can join them in the future. The avenues of time will never be so wide again." He cradled his guitar under his arm and jumped through the fire.

Robert stood still. "Do you want—?" he said to Solange. "What do you want to do?"

"I don't know," Solange said slowly. "They've won the revolution, but it's not my time. I don't know if I could, if I could start over, learn things the people of this time take for granted."

"I would love to," Robert said. "I would love to start again, to take the last great adventure. But it's almost a hundred years in the future for me. I'd be lost. And without you— Though what difference would it make? I'd be without you in any case."

"We'll see each other again," Solange said. "They can't keep us apart."

"How do you know?" Robert said. He watched the circle of fire close. Time was running out. If he could never see her again, he would wager everything, leave everything behind for the unimaginable future. "How can you be so certain?"

"Certain things defy time," she said. "Dreams,

love . . . André knows what they are. I've walked through time before for something that was important to me. I know I'll find you again."

"But when?" he asked. He was embarrassed to hear pleading in his voice. "When?"

"I don't know," she said. "You'll know when it happens, times when you'll feel the need for adventure or the marvelous— Look for me then."

He held her close, his face hidden in her wiry hair. "That'll have to do," he said. "God knows I've never asked for more certainty than that. But I'll miss you."

"I'll miss you terribly," she said. They kissed, the noises of celebration surrounding them.

The ring of fire was still there when they separated, though smaller than ever. Robert looked around, his hand holding Solange's. Jacques was backing away from the ring, shaking his head. "Not for me," he said. "I prefer my time, the familiar. For someone else, perhaps. Not me."

Antonin was sitting on the ground, his head in his hands. He shook as if crying. Perhaps he hadn't heard the black man's last words, didn't realize his chance. Louis stood awkwardly, his hand in his coat pocket. "Not for you either, eh?" he said to Robert. "Crazy place to live, all right. Who knows what'll happen there? I'd prefer going home myself. André, though, it's something André would do."

They both looked at André, who was staring at the closing ring of fire as if mesmerized. Near him Yves and Patrice stood, both shaking their heads. "Who's going to do it, I wonder?" Robert said. "Who's going to take the chance? Once I would have sworn I'd do it, sworn I'd change my life if I was given the chance, but now I don't know. My life's changed enough in the past months, enough even for me."

André shrugged almost convulsively. The ring of fire was reflected in his eyes. He jerked away, shaking. "No," he said finally. "No, who knows—?" The circle was now almost too small to fit through.

Hélène cried out suddenly. She ran to the burning ring and jumped through effortlessly. They saw her land on the other side and turn and wave. Then the ring closed.

"Hélène," Robert said. He shook his head in wonder. "Who would have thought it? Hélène, of all people."

The ground shifted underneath them. The surrealists looked around, blinking. The magic café lights of the Rue Fontaine beckoned. Solange was gone. They were back in their own time.

TEN

"There is no total revolution, there is only perpetual Revolution, real life, like love, dazzling at every moment."

Paul Eluard

Robert dressed slowly, smiling a little. Paul Eluard had written, Paul who had escaped the confines of winter and gone to Polynesia with money taken from his father's construction business. Paul was coming back today. It would be good to see him again.

"Good day," Robert said to the concierge as he came down the stairs, wondering what time it was. He had come in late again last night, slept late and then written for a few hours. Got to get my clock fixed, he thought. Someday.

"You're very cheerful today," the concierge said. "You haven't forgotten that the rent is due tomorrow, have you?"

"No, I haven't," Robert said, who had indeed forgotten and would probably forget again for several more days. "See you later."

"Good-bye," the concierge said. She withdrew into her room.

Light snow was falling, the last of the Paris winter. Robert shivered. He had left his coat somewhere again, somewhere in the summer of the next century. Soon it will be spring, he thought, feeling a connection with the changes of the seasons. Spring, and then I won't need a coat until fall. And by then something will turn up. He felt light, unburdened, happy for no reason. The lights of the Café Cyrano shone out against the darkening street.

"Robert!" someone said from inside the café. Paul had left his seat and come to meet him at the door. They embraced. "Robert, how have you been? You look good. They've been telling me a fantastic story, I don't believe a word of it . . ."

Robert sat down at the table next to Paul and ordered grenadine. "It's all true," he said. "Every word of it, even the parts they made up. But how are you? Look at you, you're so dark. How was Polynesia?"

"Wonderful," Paul said. "Marvelous. Everything I expected. Sunsets like ripe grapes, women with skin the color of brown silk . . . Travel—you forget your old life, your past. Everything you do is different, takes on a new meaning. Everything changes. Not just the obvious things like the language, the money—every gesture means something new, every color . . ."

Robert nodded, leaning forward. For one last time he saw with clarity into the future, saw that he would spend a large part of his life traveling. He would know the world as he knew Paris, would learn other ways of speaking, learn other slang, hear other music. He felt excited, excited and ready to go. Why not? He had no ties here. "Where did you go?" he said, eager to begin charting his course. "What did you see? I envy you."

Paul laughed. "Why are you so anxious to go?" he said. "André tells me you've all been having an adventure like nothing I've ever dreamed of. You especially. I can't believe I missed it. André," he said loudly, getting his attention, "Robert says it's all true. Everything you've said."

André stopped speaking and looked at Robert. "Of course it was," he said. "Everything we say here, everything we do, is true."

Robert sighed. André could never miss an opportunity for a lecture. "Naked women, skeletons," someone next to Robert was saying, "streetlamps, train stations." Robert shook off his irritation. In some ways it was good to be back.

Paul was telling a story about an Englishman he had met in Polynesia. Robert leaned back in his chair, lifting the front two legs off the floor. He looked at the faces around him, a charcoal sketch in the dim light. They were all his good friends, even Antonin. This was where the adventure had started, and this was where it should end. Perhaps he would travel the world as he foresaw, but every voyage would end here, in this café. He lifted his glass and drank, wondering why he did not feel as certain about his future as he had a moment before. But the feeling of well-being, of happiness, did not leave him.

"Did you write anything in Polynesia?" André said. "Any poems?"

"I brought back some art," Paul said. "Fantastic

stuff, I'll have to show it to you later. Masks, tribal fetishes . . . I gave my paints to one of the villagers and he drew some of the most incredible things—"

"That's because they've kept in touch with the subconscious, with their dreams," André said. "They're living a life we've lost, a life we should return to."

"Oh, I don't know," Paul said. "I wouldn't want to live the way they do, half of them dead before they're twenty. And some of the taboos, well . . ." He saw André's face and trailed off. Robert sighed again. After all these years they were still unable to challenge André.

"But you," Paul said. "I hear you've all done a lot of work. The magazine, the Bureau of Surrealistic Research—Robert, you've even sold something, haven't you? A book of poems?"

"A novel," Robert said flatly.

"A novel?" Paul said. He looked at André, then looked away. "I thought— Well, the manifesto you sent me said—"

"Robert and I had to work together in the future," André said. "We agreed to put aside our disagreements, to resolve them after the revolution was over. As I understand it, Robert, you were only working on this novel to raise money after you were disinherited . . ."

"As you understand it!" Robert said. The front two legs of his chair hit the floor loudly as he sat upright. André was giving him a way out, but he didn't care. His irritation had grown while André was speaking and now had finally spilled over. Someone should challenge André, someone should confront him after all these years, and it looked as though it would be he. Without stopping to think, he went on. "When have you ever understood anything? When have you ever listened to anyone besides yourself and your endless theories and manifestos? I've told you, I've told you over and over again that

Lisa Goldstein

I'm writing novels because I want to write novels, that nothing you can say will convince me that I want to write anything besides novels. Do you really think I want to spend my life writing down my dreams and making up that drivel you call poetry? Anyone can do that, a child can do that, probably better than you can."

All around him faces were turning to him in shock. He knew he had gone too far, said some things he did not even mean, but it was too late. Someone across the table nervously dropped a glass and Robert remembered the last time—it seemed years and years ago—someone had dropped a glass at this table, Antonin's poem.

André looked at Robert, blue-green eyes like ice. "That is just the point," he said. Robert could see that he was making a great attempt to keep from shouting. "That is the point exactly. A child could do it. That is what we hope to achieve here, to achieve childhood. That is what you will never—"

Robert did not let him finish. "I've achieved it just as much as you have," he said. "I've written poems that have taken me three seconds to write—everyone here at this table has seen me write them. What does that prove—that my mind is like a little child's, or that anyone no matter who he is can write drivel like that?" He knew that there could never be an apology enormous enough for what he had just said. He didn't care. He was tired of people who told him what state his soul was in, André and Antonin and a few of the others who took their cue from André. He had gone through something, something so strange that even now he was not sure what it meant, but he knew he was somehow stronger for it. He would not give that up to be a follower again.

"It's obvious that you don't understand anything about what surrealism is—" André said, still controlled.

"Who is that obvious to?" Robert said, furious now. "You? What if I told you I think I'm more of a surrealist than you'll ever be? I've lived my life, I've done everything I wanted and I'm not even thirty yet. You're the one who's always telling us to follow our desires—well, right now my desires tell me I don't want to stay in this movement any more. That I don't want to be a follower any more, of anything. Why do you think you didn't stay in the future, didn't stay in your ideal world when you had the chance?"

"Why didn't you?" André said. His composure was beginning to break.

"That's not what I asked," Robert said. "Because Paris is my home, this time is my home. But you— you've dreamed of that world all your life and do you know why you didn't go?"

"I don't care—" André said, but Robert would not let him finish.

"Because you could never live in a world with no leaders, could never live where you weren't the leader," Robert said. "You—"

"Why don't you just leave right now then, if that's—" André said. His eyes flashed. He had never been this angry with Robert, but Robert knew from experience that he had good reason to be terrified. He took a deep breath to calm himself.

"Quiet," Robert said. He could hear people breathing around the table but no one said anything. Good, he thought. Maybe they'll learn something from this. "I've been meaning to tell you this for seven years. Eight. You've found—discovered—something wonderful, something unique, something probably unheard of in our civilization for thousands of years. And then you patent it, don't let it out of your sight, make a mockery of people who don't have your version of the one real truth. You set yourself up as a leader of an idea that should be free to all, that rejects the very concept of leaders and followers. You've been appointed caretaker of a strange, fragile flower, and you've botched it."

Robert turned to go. Complete silence had fallen over the group. He could hear the waiters in the kitchen calling out orders, the clink of glasses at the other tables. He left the café. No one called after him.

Later that night he woke out of a dream to hear knocking at his door. "Who—" he said, getting up and wrapping the blanket around him. The floor was bitter cold to his bare feet. "Who is it?" he said.

"It's me," Paul said. "Let me in, for God's sake."

Robert opened the door. Paul stood outside, holding a bottle by the neck. He was alone. "It's freezing out here," Paul said, shivering. "Should have stayed where I was."

"Come in, come in," Robert said. "It's freezing in here too."

Paul handed him the bottle. "Bad champagne," he said. "The only thing I could steal as we were leaving."

Robert looked at him questioningly. "Times are rough," Paul said, trying to smile. He sat down in the room's only chair. "Dad says he wants the money back. All of it."

"So?" Robert said. "Hold on, I'll get you a glass." He found two mismatched glasses and poured the champagne, then sat back on the bed.

"I'll probably have to go to work for him again," Paul said. "It's awful—I don't think I can face it." Suddenly he smiled. "Would you like a street named after you? I could probably manage it."

"Have you talked to anyone else?" Robert said. "Maybe you could get a job somewhere else. Have you talked to Louis?"

"Maybe," Paul said. He drank his champagne thoughtfully. "Maybe I'll just go back to Polynesia. Things weren't as complicated."

They sat for a while in silence. "How did you get past the concierge?" Robert asked finally.

Paul laughed. "Told her it was an emergency," he said.

Robert laughed with him. "I thought André threw me out," he said. "I wonder if you're even allowed to visit me."

Paul shrugged. "Oh, that's just André," he said. "He'll take you back after he's had a while to think about it. After all, you've known him—how long now? Seven years?"

"Eight," Robert said. "But— I don't know—this time I don't think I want to come back. He threw me out once before, you know. While you were gone."

Paul raised his eyebrows. "Maybe that was the dress rehearsal," Robert said. "I think this is the real thing. I'm tired of being told what to do, Paul. What to think, how to react."

"Well," Paul said. He poured another glass of champagne. "We'll all come visit you, anyway. Things won't change that much."

"All of you except André," Robert said. He shook his head. "How do you say good-bye to your best friend? If only he weren't so stubborn. It's like getting a divorce."

"Oh, come on, it's not that bad," Paul said. Robert had to smile. Paul had come to be cheered up and had ended up instead trying to cheer him up. "André says you met a beautiful woman while I was gone—what was her name?"

"Solange," Robert said. "Met her and lost her again."

"Oh," Paul said. "I'm sorry. André didn't tell me that."

"André didn't know," Robert said. "Maybe— I don't know. Maybe I didn't lose her. She's— Well, she's not easy to get hold of. She's from the future."

"First André and now you," Paul said. "Sooner or later I'm going to believe you really did go to the future."

"Believe it or not, I don't care," Robert said. "That's where I met her. She's in her time and I'm in mine. She said—she said we'd meet again—somehow—somehow walk through the avenues of time—" He drank the last of his champagne and poured another glass. "But that hasn't happened yet."

"And you think it won't?" Paul said.

"No," Robert said. "I think it will. I know it will. It's just sometimes—the waiting—"

Paul was looking at him strangely. "God!" he said finally. "If only—if only you knew. It's the perfect love story. You'll never grow complacent, or grow used to each other. Never argue about money, or what's for dinner. Every day will be exciting, because that's the day you might meet her. Every place you go will have a new meaning, because that's the place she might be. She'll transform the world for you, until you fall in love with the world. And each time you meet her it will almost be like meeting her for the first time."

"You don't know," Robert said. "If you had to do it—"

Paul studied him for a moment. "I'd trade places with you in a second," he said. "You've discovered a way to make love last forever and you complain. You were right when you argued with André at the café today. You are a true surrealist. Because of Solange you'll never be able to become a part of the middle class, to marry and have a family—" He looked at Robert shrewdly. "And you never wanted to, isn't that right?"

"No," said Robert slowly. "I want—I think I want to travel."

"Well," Paul said. "I've been traveling, but I haven't had half the strange experiences you've had. And yours are just beginning. You said to me at the café today that you envied me, but I think that if I envied anyone it would be you. Don't you realize what kind of a chance you have?"

Robert nodded slowly. A conviction that Paul was right grew within him, and with it his old desire to encounter marvels. He saw himself meeting Solange, an endless series of meetings like a hall of mirrors. And each time they met they would tell each other their adventures and fall in love all over again until it was time to go back. Nothing ever ends, he thought. You think you know what your life will be like thirty years from now and suddenly you're doing something you couldn't have planned five minutes ago. It's the people who have settled down, even people like André, who are dead. And me—I'm alive. I have to be, because at any moment I might meet her again. "You're right," he said to Paul. He clicked his glass against Paul's in a toast. "Here's to impermanence," he said.

ABOUT THE AUTHOR

Lisa Goldstein is one of a new generation of writers challenging the boundaries between fantasy and realism. In addition to her debut novel, *The Red Magician*, she is also the author of several highly praised short stories. She is married and currently living in Northern California.